An Easter Egg Hunt

Gillian Freeman is the author of nine novels and three non-fiction books. She is an accomplished screen writer and has also written the scenarios for two full-length Kenneth MacMillan ballets; *Mayerling* and *Isadora*. *That Cold Day in the Park* was one of her films and was directed by Robert Altman. She is married to Edward Thorpe, ballet critic and author. They live in Highgate and have two daughters.

Gillian Freeman

An Easter Egg Hunt

Pavanne
published by Pan Books

First published 1981 by Hamish Hamilton Ltd
This Pavanne edition published 1982 by Pan Books Ltd,
Cavaye Place, London SW10 9PG
© Gillian Freeman 1981
ISBN 0 330 26800 7
Printed and bound in Great Britain by
Hunt Barnard Printing, Aylesbury, Bucks

For Paula And David Swift

Part One

An Easter Egg Hunt

The following short story was first published in *An Argosy of Mystery Tales*, Christmas 1917.

A Strange Disappearance

This is a true story which is why, unlike so many fictional confections, it offers no definitive conclusion to its mystery. Perhaps the Reader will take on the detective's role and discover a vital clue overlooked by the Author who, convinced that those who were involved will not fail to recognize the originals and even now come forward, has taken it upon himself to alter the names of people and places. Had Madeleine disappeared at any time other than War there would have been wider concern, but more monumental events naturally took precedence in the newspaper columns. The episode merited only a few short paragraphs here and there and was soon forgotten – much to the relief of Madame Marie Pennington, Principal of the Academy for Young Ladies at Fairwater House.

Whether Madame Pennington was a true widow and whether she had ever passed more than an afternoon at the Sorbonne gave rise to lively conversations in the neighbouring villages of Fairwater Edge and Fairwater Green. Certainly she was French-spoken, certainly she had lived with Major Pennington as his wife until he died in 1911. Certainly his fortune, if there was one, had been willed elsewhere. Everyone knew that she had been left with a mansion and no money to run it, with a clutch of local servants who gossiped because they could not be paid. When the brass plaque went up beside the ornate wrought-iron gates and it was observed that she was no longer to be addressed as 'Mrs', Lady Reed, whose own origins were obscure, pronounced her indisputably bourgeois and unfit to run a school. Doctor Robert Ford, who had attended the Major until his end, thought it damned courageous of her to embark on such an undertaking, and the Reverend Burder gave it his blessing and promised that when *his* girls were ready to be finished he would not send them elsewhere. It was common knowledge that his stipend would never run to the fees and that it was Mrs Burder, with an income of her own, who would make the decision.

An advertisement in *The Times*, a mention in the late Major Pennington's Regimental Gazette, brought six girls the first term to Fairwater House. Betty, Dolly and Gladys were officer's daughters, home from India now for good, since Dolly's mother had recently died there and Betty's skin and Gladys's stomach reacted severely to the heat. Gertie's father was in the Colonial Service; her mother considered manners decidedly too rough in their outpost for an only daughter. Phyllis and Millie, sisters were the first of their family to benefit from the lucrative corrective corset invented and patented by their father, by profession an engineer.

'My pioneers,' Madam Pennington called them as they gathered together on the platform at Euston Station, the girls in their long navy blue uniform cloaks, Madame in well-cut maroon cloth tailored in Fairwater Green by a dressmaker who, she said, 'had, for an Englishwoman, extraordinary flair.'

This was the nucleus, then, which multiplied threefold before Madeleine presented herself at the school in the late September of 1914. As it happened the six were also to become her closest confidantes – or so each of them thought. (Florrie, whose devotion was the greatest, came later, after Madeleine herself.)

She was the daughter of Madame's cousin, this much they knew as they watched Madeleine's arrival from the dining room window. The chauffeur-driven Sunbeam tourer ('Hired!' said Gertie) drew up before the main door, frightening Doctor Ford's horse as he trotted it down the drive. ('He has to be sweet on Madame,' said Phyllis, 'always calling, even when no one is ill.')

The chauffeur handed out a woman first, small, stout and from what they could see beneath the veil, with features similar to Madame Pennington's own. The girl who followed was tall and slender. Her mole-grey coat was buttoned to the neck and, like the older woman, she wore hat and gloves to match. They waited a few moments while the chauffeur unstrapped the small trunk, then they walked together to the house, out of sight of the excited girls. They heard the bell ring and then the parlourmaid's heavy step in the hall. (She was in a temper and had handed in her notice but they knew nothing of that.)

It was Betty who was summoned by Madame to take Madeleine round the school, Betty who reported to the other five that Madeleine had crossed the Channel only the day before and was to stay for the duration of hostilities, was to teach French conversation but take part in lessons herself, was to sleep in the four-bedded Pink Dormitory but was to have special privileges in accordance with her age. 'She's seventeen – and *incredibly* beautiful.'

In due course plain, bespectacled Florrie made a secret oath to capture that beauty with her new Box Brownie. She was the only girl at the Academy to have seen a moving picture and was planning to be the first of her sex to rival Mr Griffith. If he inspired the long-term ambition, love and admiration for Madeleine was her source for the present. She 'snapped' Madeleine in the art room as she decorated eggs for the charity Easter Egg Hunt (more delicately painted, more artistically designed than anything created by other girls); she 'snapped' her again at the lakeside on Easter Sunday before breakfast, probably, as the police officer told her sternly as he studied the blurred results, the last person to see here before . . . well, before whatever happened to her took place.

It was on that Sunday, 4 April 1915, that this strange story began.

* * * *

At seven fifteen or thereabouts on Easter morning, Millie, the prefect in charge, withdrew the long bolt that fastened the garden door and led the girls out into the early mist. There were, perhaps, a dozen of them, those with parents abroad or with homes disrupted by the war. The rest had departed for the holidays and were, so Gertie said enviously, now in the bosoms of their families eating decent roast beef and sleeping in comfortable beds.

From the kitchen doorway Cook watched them as they collected the painted eggshells from the table where they had placed them in preparation the previous night. There were to be scrambled eggs for breakfast (Madame's orders), but it wasn't Cook's way of doing things and she hoped they hadn't gone off, being blown into a bowl all those hours before.

Madeleine was the last to leave, holding her cloak closely round her as if she were cold and loath to go out of doors. Through the kitchen window one of the scullery maids, Ida, saw her walk swiftly across the wet grass, saw Florrie with her camera set off in pursuit. (If Cook had not at that moment chivvied her to set the tables, what else might she have had to tell the young policeman as he spooned with her late that night?)

The gardens of Fairwater House sloped down to the lake. Major Pennington had claimed fishing rights, invoking the title deeds, then regretted it, for they showed them to be vested for all time in the Crown. Just as the lake was out of bounds to fishermen, so was the lake path to the girls. Narrow, sandy, it followed the water's edge to where a rocky incline concealed it from the house above and erosion had formed cave-like openings where spiders nested and bats hung. Beyond was a gate where the grass was so long and thick it opened barely wide enough for Ida to pass through as she came to work each morning at half past five, but this was the ancient footpath from Fairwater Green and gave her extra time in bed. The lane, which was easier underfoot, took a circuitous route, cutting through woodland and skirting fields.

Ida yawned as she struck the breakfast gong and thought it was unfair that she should be made to work on a Holy Day when her sisters were still lying in bed. The girls came in and Gladys smiled at her, but the others went by chattering as if she wasn't there. They told each other of their cleverness in concealing the eggs, how invisible they appeared among the pebbles edging the path in the ornamental rockery, under the clipped hedges and in the fretwork on the summer hou. They hung their cloaks on the row of pegs, then filed into the dining room, hungry after their excursion in the chill morning air. They wore their Sunday dresses with Puritan collars, very white and stiff with starch. It made one hold one's neck as stiff as a ruler, Phyllis complained, unless one wanted to be garotted by one's own frock, but it pleased pretty Miss Cadogan who had joined the school that year. Her province was deportment, but Madame knew that if she were to continue to draw pupils she must keep among the *avant garde*, and Miss Cadogan was modern enough not only to be skilled at hockey but had also had the privilege of seeing Miss Isadora Duncan dance. She had versed herself in the art of Greek Movement, and in her teaching tunic of flowing silk, a filet binding her hair, she presented a romantic figure to the girls, as romantic as tall, gentle Miss Darke who read poetry so thrillingly to the senior class. The two women came into breakfast together and stood behind their chairs. They had attended early service at Fairwater Parish Church. Miss Craig came next, elderly and severe and as unyielding as the mathematical principles she strove to inculcate. She walked with a firm step, defying the rheumatic pain that knifed her knee. Matron followed with Madame, and they took their places. Madame surveyed the room, made her choice.

'Gertie Davies, will you say grace for us this morning, please.'

'For - what - we - are - about - to - receive - may - the - Lord - make - us-truly-thankful-for-Jesus-Christ's-sake,' muttered Gertie, who hated to be singled out for anything.

Next to her Gladys repressed a giggle. Solemn occasions, even the familiar ritual of grace, always affected her this way.

The staff took their seats, and there followed the scraping of chairs as the girls sat, too. The mistresses were placed only along one side of their table, ostensibly to watch the behaviour and correct the table manners of their charges, but Dolly insisted that Madame liked the view of the front drive so that if the Doctor called her blushes would be over before she received him. Millie believed the staff table was where it was solely because of its proximity to the sideboard. Food was invariably cold by the time it reached the end of the room.

The parlourmaid had not been replaced. The young women of Fairwater had found new freedom in serving the Tommies in canteens. Ida had therefore donned a cap and apron, scrubbed her red hands, and now arrived from the kitchen with a dish which contained portions of scrambled egg on toast slices under a metal dome. The second scullery maid, a much simpler-minded girl by chance named Ada which gave rise to jokes both found wearisome, followed with a tray of pots of tea. It was not until the food was served and Madame was on the point of putting a sugar lump into her cup that she saw that Madeleine's chair was empty. She drew Matron's attention to it.

'When you have finished eating . . . no please, not before . . . perhaps you would slip upstairs and see if she is feeling unwell.'

The girls, too, were curious, and with it excited, as girls generally are in circumstances which draw on their speculation.

'Did you see her come in?' 'Did you see her go out?' 'Perhaps she is ill.'

'Ill?' said Gertie. '*She* hasn't eaten these eggs.' The witticism was passed by each girl to her neighbour until they were all in fits. Dolly waited until they had subsided. Then she spoke very quietly.

'I heard her crying last night.'

She commanded silence. They looked at one another. Florrie said defensively, 'Well, wouldn't you be homesick in a foreign country? Her father's probably dead.'

'It's funny, but I never think of England as foreign,' said Betty. 'Even in India the natives think of it as home.'

They argued the point hotly, contrasting the loyalties of Empire and France, until Florrie pointed out that Matron had left the table, and they wondered if she had been stricken by the same malaise that had kept Madeleine from breakfast (homesickness had by now been ruled out), or whether she had gone to search, or whether it had by now been discovered that Rosemary Whitaker had spilt ink on her sheet.

Madeleine had not been upstairs. Matron had looked not only in the Pink Dormitory, but in the others as well. She had climbed to the Art Room on the top floor and made certain that she was not in such unlikely places as the linen room or even in the closet Madame had allowed Florrie to turn into a darkroom, a concession resented by several of the girls. ('We encourage hobbies,' Madame told parents, and when Florrie's father, who was in the government, had drawn attention to his daughter's passion, this was the deciding factor in sending her to the school.)

Madeleine's cloak was not on its peg, nor her walking shoes in their locker, and by the time the crocodile had been formed for the walk to Church, Madame was attempting to reassure herself that when they reached it, Madeleine (who had these privileges after all) would be waiting in her pew. She addressed the girls nevertheless.

'Before we set off I have an announcement to make. I have asked Cook to arrange a cold luncheon.' (There was a concerted groan.) 'Yes, I know it is Sunday, but it is also Easter Sunday and the kitchen staff want to attend the church service as much as you do.' (As if summoned by a cue Cook and the scullery maids came out of the door wearing their coats and hats.) 'Also, it is the day of our Easter Egg Hunt and our grounds will be open to the villagers early this afternoon. I want the meal eaten and cleared as rapidly as possible.' She paused, pressed the tips of her gloved fingers together. 'Has anyone seen Madeleine this morning?'

The girls looked at each other. Florrie put up her hand. 'Yes, Florrie?'

'I saw her when we were hiding the eggs.'

Madame said impatiently, 'But not since?'

'No, Madame.'

'Who is her walking partner this morning?' Phyllis put up her hand this time. 'Very well, Phyllis, you will come with me.' She walked with Phyllis to the front of the crocodile and they started off down the drive.

As they approached the curve by the hockey field, Phyllis cast a frantic look over her shoulder at the girls behind. A kind of *frisson* went through the little procession and one or two glanced up to the tops of the tall trees where pieces of torn silk protruded like blossom among the new leaves.

'Cross your fingers,' whispered Florrie to Gladys, her partner. In front of them Dolly stared straight ahead.

'Did you really see it?' Ada asked Ida, for both believed implicitly in ghosts.

'That poor boy,' said Miss Cadogan to Miss Darke. 'Every time I pass I think of the wasted young life.'

'Well,' Miss Darke answered, 'one has to look at it this way. He was as likely to die in combat if he had survived the training. I'm afraid our fliers stand little chance.'

'I know,' said Miss Cadogan, 'but I wish we could have been spared the experience. The girls . . .' and they both looked along the double row of heads to where Dolly's thick fair plait identified her among the identical velour hats. Dolly, as everyone now knew, had been the most affected by the tragic disaster. As if in acknowledgement of the sentiment there was a tearing sound in the branches, and a small portion of splintered wood from the tail empennage of the wrecked biplane fell through the foliage and lodged again a few feet below.

Had the colloquial 'bird's eye view' become a human possibility that Sunday, it would have been observed that almost equidistant to the parish church, but from opposite directions, came the girls from Fairwater House and the cadet squad from the Royal Flying Corps barracks on the outskirts of Fairwater Edge. Neither saw the approach of the other until they converged at the churchyard gate (for the church stood at the cross-roads) but the sound of marching feet had reached the ears of Madame Pennington's charges and the thrill of apprehension passed among them.

'Eyes right,' murmured Gertie to Millie, because they were not permitted to look openly. Only Ida, who considered herself free from such rules, frankly stared.

'You may break rank, girls. Go in quietly,' said Madame who was anxious to have them safely inside and facing the pulpit. At that moment the bell-ringers concluded their final peal.

'Flight – Flight halt! Stand at ease! Stand easy!' shouted the Warrant Officer as the school party filed through the gate. Gertie could not resist a quick glance back at the sound of the motor-car engine. She wondered if it would ever be considered ladylike to drive.

'Come along, Gertie!' She just caught a glimpse of the Vauxhall 'Prince Henry' (she could, at least, recognize the different body designs even if she could not take the wheels) before she crossed from the sunlight into the gloom of the porch.

The car drew up alongside the cadets. In the front seat was a uniformed driver, in the rear a colonel accompanied by a younger officer.* The driver climbed down and opened the small rear door.

'Flight . . . at ease! Flight . . . attention!' shouted the Warrant Officer, and the Colonel inspected the squad. 'Flight . . . left turn! Flight . . . caps off! . . . Flight . . . forward march!' His voice was heard above the organ and

---

* At the time the events took place the Royal Flying Corps – an integral part of the army – used military titles to denote rank.

although the girls dared not turn their heads they were aware of the young men edging into the pews behind them.

Before the service began Matron passed each of them a threepenny piece for the Collection. Dolly, who was developing views of her own, whispered, 'The price of a place in heaven!' which shocked the girl at her side. When the choir entered (eight small boys and four men, two of whom were the vergers) she experienced a sense of antagonism she was not able to explain, as though she were imprisoned like brave ardent Bonnivard in Chillon (Miss Darke had been reading Bryon to them), while Madeleine had somehow managed to throw off the yoke and escape. It isn't fair, thought Dolly. The Vicar said: 'Christ is risen from the dead, and became the first-fruits of them that slept.'

In the pause that followed, there was the sound of the heavy iron latch of the door opening, and along with everybody else Dolly turned her head to see who was causing this distraction. She saw that it was Doctor Ford who, without looking about him, went straight to his pew and knelt, covering his face and the dreadful jagged war scar with his hands. Matron tapped her sharply on the shoulder with her hymn book. 'Turn round at once!' and Dolly did as she was told thinking how pale and exhausted he looked and imagined that he had been tending a patient through the night. She found the medical profession noble but was beginning to have her doubts about the clergy.

'When the wicked man turneth away from his wickedness that he hath committed, and doeth that which is lawful and right he shall save his soul alive,' boomed Mr Burder. He is so old-fashioned, thought Dolly, who was herself moving into the New Age, so Victorian. Does he really bring comfort? 'Oh Lord,' he said, 'we beseech thy blessing for two sons of this Parish, John Edward Wood aged nineteen years and Walter Frederick John Palmer, eighteen years, who lay down their lives for this country, and for God.' Across the aisle a man was crying. 'They were as healthy branches of the English oak,' improvised the Vicar, 'torn asunder in the storm which ravages our land.'

18

'They didn't die in *our* land,' whispered Florrie. 'More like Madeleine's land.'

'He's being symbolic,' Gertie whispered back. 'Oh, Florrie, where do you think she is?'

Miss Craig hissed at them to stop talking, in a voice loud enough for Madame to hear so that later they were bound to be in trouble (Why is it, Gertie said on the way back, that I always get picked on and Gladys, who put a farthing in the plate and pocketed her threepence, gets away scot-free?)

The service ended. The man who had been crying blew his nose hard with a comic trumpeting noise, and as the Reverend Burder stepped down from the pulpit ready to dispense compassion, Doctor Ford stood up and without looking left or right hurried out of the church. Madame Pennington, who had been anxious to talk to him, pretended she had not seen his departure but was busy with the buttons on her gloves.

Madame opened her bureau and took out the tortoise-shell cigarette box that she had given the Major for his fifty-fourth birthday. (He had died at the early age of fifty-six.) On the front of the box was a silver scroll with his initials and the date, inside were the cigarettes that had been especially rolled for her in Fairwater Green. She was on the point of opening the lid to take one when there was a knock on the study door. She thrust the box back into the bureau, turned her back to it and called out, 'Entrez!' It was Miss Cadogan who came in.

'You almost caught me,' said Madame with relief. 'I thought it was one of the girls.' She took the box out again and this time offered it to Miss Cadogan. 'Will you join me?'

'Thank you.' Miss Cadogan took a cigarette and looked at it appreciatively.

'Please,' said Madame. 'Do sit down.' She took her own silver cigarette holder from a pigeon-hole and handed an amber one to Miss Cadogan. She tried to sound in control but her voice was tremulous and to her humiliation her eyes filled with tears. 'Where is Madeleine, do you think?'

Miss Cadogan sat down on a high-backed chair. She always disdained the ones which made you slump. 'She wouldn't do anything daft, would she?'

Madame disliked the use of the word. Miss Cadogan had so many virtues, but she had a bluntness of speech which one could only hope was not picked up by the girls.

'You mean like try and swim the Channel to France? Try and get on a troop ship?'

Madame shook her head. 'We had a long talk about her parents and their situation. She was, as she always is, extremely sensible.'

Miss Cadogan thought Madeleine was far from sensible but it was not her place to say so. 'May I have a light, Madame?'

'Oh, I am so sorry. The disappearance has made me distrait . . . ' She took a box of Swan Vesta matches from the bureau and struck several before she obtained a light. 'No,' she said, continuing her thought. 'I do not believe she would be so foolish.' She paused. 'But she is not in the school.'

'Are you sure?' Miss Cadogan drew on her cigarette, savouring the flavour and wondering why Madame bothered to go through the ritual and yet not once put the holder anywhere near her lips.

'Why should she hide? We have looked in all the possible places.' She tapped the ash into the small silver tray. 'I am afraid she may have hurt herself in the grounds.'

'I'll go and have a look,' Miss Cadogan volunteered as the gong sounded. 'If you will excuse me from the dining room, that is.'

Madame put out her cigarette and reluctantly Miss Cadogan did the same. Madame emptied the ashtray into the grate. 'I'll ask Cook to leave you a plate in the pantry,' she said. 'I am most grateful.' She took the teacher's hands and pressed them. She was not generally so demonstrative but there was an ominous feeling in the region of her heart.

Miss Darke said grace. 'Benedicus Benedicat.'

There were two empty places this lunchtime.

'They're not missing anything!' grumbled Gertie, looking distastefully at the cold ham and tongue on her plate. The slices had curled a little at the edges and the mashed potato that Sylvia was passing her had visible greyish lumps. As for the water jugs, she could tell they had been filled before they went to church for there were bubbles all round the inside of the glass.

Miss Cadogan wondered where she should look first and decided on the spinney. She was not sure what she expected to find, but being an admirer of the work of Sir Arthur Conan Doyle, murder had crossed her mind. She knew of one person at least who had reason to hate Madeleine, but she had to admit that violence seemed out of character. Curiously, she was not alarmed at the prospect of discovering a body. Lately she had come to regard death in an entirely new light, due to Miss Darke who embraced a kind of pantheism she had managed to reconcile with traditional Christianity. They attended services together, but from time to time, in the moonlight, recited poetry and experienced a sense of comfort from the proximity of nature. Miss Cadogan entered the thicket of trees and, keeping to the paths, scanned the growth on either side. She saw a rabbit and a great many birds and what seemed to her a prodigious amount of last autumn's dead leaves that had not returned to the soil, but there was no sign of Madeleine, dead or alive. She was beginning to wish that she had not offered to make her search before eating lunch. She emerged from the spinney and crossed the lawn and the sight of Cook behind the kitchen window stimulated a slight peckishness into recognizable hunger.

'Two portions, Mrs Parsons, then,' said Madame, as the scullery maids put dishes of pink blancmange on trays. The figure of Miss Cadogan, in wellington boots and mackintosh, passed the window and trudged purposefully down towards the lake.

'I won't be here, Madam,' said Cook firmly. (Nothing would make her use a Frenchified pronounciation.) 'I've made arrangements to visit my sister's family in Little Stratton.'

'I wasn't for one moment suggesting that you should stay,' said Madame. 'I was only asking you to cover two plates of cold meats and leave them on the pantry shelf. Puddings too, please.'

'I've always had Easter Sunday afternoon off,' Cook went on as though she were being obstructed. 'I hope you don't think I'm neglecting my duties.'

Madame sighed. 'Of course not. Miss Cadogan and Madeleine will be eating late, that is all.'

Cook had served at Fairwater House when the principal was merely the Major's wife and was not taken in by the casual manner. She had observed Mrs Pennington's behaviour through a number of crises. 'She's not turned up then?' she asked, reflecting her employer's tone. She added, 'She looked pale when she went out this morning. She hasn't been too well, has she, pulled down . . .?'

'Oh, Mrs Parsons,' said Madame, her defences demolished. 'I'm worried to distraction. Did she say anything to you, give any indication . . .?'

Cook was aware that her scullery maids were standing there with laden trays, agog with interest. 'There's young ladies in there, waiting for their blancmanges!' she said sharply, and when they had gone through the baize-covered door into the dining room, she turned back to Madame. 'We had our usual joke, that's all. Miss Madeleine said good morning to me and I said "Bon jour!" to her. . . .'

'Nothing else?'

'I told her she'd better hurry or she'd be late for breakfast. The others had all gone ahead, you see. She said she wasn't hungry so I said the air would give her an appetite. Begging your pardon, Madam,' Cook concluded deferentially, 'but the French don't seem to take to the fresh air.'

Madeleine had been persuaded to paint the poster for the

Easter Egg Hunt. Always modest, she had at first demurred, suggesting Millie or Gertie for the task. They too urged Madeleine, saying that her abilities, her eye for colour, her lettering outshone everyone else's, until at last she had agreed but only if they promised honest criticism. She was not offended by rejection, she was willing to try and try again if necessary. Of course it was not. The poster was arresting, brilliant and *artistic*. Gertie's eyes filled with tears as she carried it down the drive to place it on the open gate. She was terribly afraid for her missing friend, bewildered by the unexplained absence and imagining her lying injured, perhaps unconscious, even dying. Dolly had hinted that Madeleine had run away, but Gertie knew that Madeleine would never cause deliberate anguish. She was too thoughtful, too sweet-natured and too grateful to Madame for giving her a home in the tranquillity of the English countryside. Gertie had defended her hotly but Dolly had actually had the nerve to smile, as if she knew Madeleine better than Gertie did – which wasn't true. No, some accident had occurred when they were hiding the eggs. Madeleine may have wandered too far, slipped and fallen, stumbled into a poacher's trap, been kicked by a horse, knocked down by a motor vehicle. Footsteps ran after Gertie and for a glorious moment she believed that Madeleine had been found and someone had been sent to tell her, but as she turned she saw it was only Millie with some extra cord to fasten the poster securely.

Gertie said, 'You're mad to run. If you're seen you'll get an order mark.'

'No one can see me. Anyway, Miss Darke sent me after you.' Millie slackened her pace. 'Listen, has it occurred to you . . . *white slave traffic.*'

'You mean someone *kidnapped* her?'

'Yes.'

'Oh, Millie!' Gertie felt quite drained and for a few seconds was unable to take a step. 'We should never see her again.'

'It still goes on a lot, you know. My uncle was telling

some friends, they rather forgot I was in the room. It isn't just the poorer sort of girl they're after. My uncle said he knew a barrister whose daughter disappeared from a teashop. From under her chaperon's eyes!'

'What shall we do?' Gertie clung to Millie's arm. 'We should tell Madame.'

'How can we?' asked Millie helplessly. 'We'd get into dreadful trouble even for thinking it. Don't you remember what happened when Phyllis asked about Antony and Cleopatra. Miss Craig put her on silence for a whole day.'

They continued down to the gates and opened them wide. Most people would be arriving on foot this afternoon, but the Vicar drove a pony trap. Gertie hung Madeleine's poster upon one of the spiked supports, her heart heavy. 'If only she were here to see it,' she said, and stepped out into the lane to obtain the full effect of the carefully drawn basket of decorated eggs (Madeleine had cleverly incorporated her own), and the contrastingly strong calligraphy reading 'Easter Egg Hunt' with the smaller letters underneath 'with prizes.' On the last line, in alternate colours of red, white and blue, were the words 'In aid of the Prisoners of War Parcels Fund. Admission one penny.'

'Wouldn't it be wonderful,' Gertie said, 'if she were back at school now, eating her lunch?'

'I just hope she's not lying bound in some ship's hold,' said Millie gloomily, although Gertie thought she discerned an element of relish in her tone.

Directly the meal was over and Gertie dispatched with the poster to the gates, the preparation for the Hunt began. Miss Darke, often so gloriously dreamy (it was what Gladys most admired in her), revealed that other aspect of her dual nature and became an organizing tyrant. Betty was so nervous she fumbled with the catch on the folding table and it collapsed on the gravel. ('Lucky the lemonade wasn't on it,' said Phyllis, helping her to set it up under Miss Darke's scornful gaze.)

Millie and Dolly were to be in charge of the takings and

had cut a slot for the pennies in a tea tin. Betty and Phyllis had the baskets, (the table was up now, and covered by a pretty white cloth), each with a label tied to its handle for the competitor's name. Florrie was in charge of the prizes. The first was a provision hamper with eggs – duck as well as chicken – a Simnel cake and pots of apricot, greengage and raspberry jam. The second prize was a single cake, a currant one with a crusty top; a box of Rowntree's chocolates was the third. 'Scrumptious!' said Florrie as she took a photograph. She intended to record a great deal on this extraordinary day. There was a booby prize, too, she almost forget it, a basket of six hard-boiled eggs. 'Too good for a booby prize,' commented Miss Darke, giving Florrie's display a mental tick. 'A very pleasing arrangement, nevertheless.' Alone among the staff members she appreciated Florrie's peculiarities, recognizing elements of herself when very young, although, of course, Florrie had not been favoured with good looks. Miss Darke admired herself and spent many hours before her glass.

Along the paths and lanes the villagers of Fairwater Edge and Fairwater Green converged upon the school. The children walked in groups, neatly dressed in their Sunday clothes, cut-down trousers pressed by hot irons, jackets patched, caps on straight; the girls wore bonnets and summer straws and tam o'shanters and everyone had shoes on their feet in deference to God and Madame and the young ladies. Poor Edwin Reed, the 'loony', overtook them all on his Victorian bicycle, and one small boy hurled a stone. His sister checked him. Edwin Reed was a gentleman even if he was do lally, Lady Reed's only son and heir to the estate.

'He frightens me,' said Gladys, posted with Gertie at the gates. 'He stares so. He even stares in church.'

'He can't speak properly,' Gertie answered severely, 'so you should feel sorry for him.' She too felt uneasy in Edwin's presence but it was her duty to keep it to herself. It didn't do to give in to one's fears. Edwin made glottal noises as he rattled past them on his hard tyres. His face was long and brownish-yellow, some said from jaundice, others from Lady Reed's sojourn in India. His tongue was always flicking beyond his lips, in and out like a lizard's. His suit had come from London and his boots shone but the handkerchief that was placed in his top pocket was far from clean.

'He watches all the time,' said Gladys.

'Of course he does,' snapped Gertie. 'So do we all. So do you.'

Gladys shook her head. 'He watched us this morning when we left the school. I saw him in the copse.'

'You couldn't have,' said Gertie, 'because he was in church with his mother. You imagined it, Gladys. You're a silly girl.' Gertie was Gladys's senior by two and three-quarter years.

The Vicar came next with his wife and children in his pony trap.

'Sarah, isn't it?' called the Vicar cheerfully.

'Gladys.'

'Gladys. Thank you for opening up the gates.' They clattered through, the pony too fat in the sides to be pulling the combined weight of the Burder family. The Vicar's son stuck out his tongue at Gladys and Gertie. 'Like an urchin!' said Gertie, shocked. She observed that the Vicar's youngest daughter shrank up against the side of the trap as it passed beneath the haunted tree. A slight breeze had set the silk fragments stirring.

Madame had been unable to eat more than a few mouthfuls of her first course and the blancmange, slippery as it was, would not go down her throat which seemed to have narrowed in direct relation to her increasing anxiety. She could think only of Madeleine and of breaking some dreadful news to her cousin. Even the prospect of that was fraught with complications. There had been no letters for the past two months, the fighting front was, as far as she could tell, beyond the town. Madeleine's father was on active service and might be wounded or dead. How ironic it was that until today Madame's dread had been of informing Madeleine that a tragedy had befallen her parents.

She allowed Miss Darke to take over the organization and hurried to her study. She locked her door and took a cigarette. She did not enjoy smoking, she had never overcome a repugnance of unladylike behaviour, but Doctor Ford had impressed upon her the need to do so to calm her nerves. She did indeed seem more tranquil, but perhaps it was the slowing down it imposed on her natural restlessness, her quick movements. 'Your Gallic qualities,' the Major used to say admiringly, for he had found them charming.

When Madame felt sufficiently composed she went downstairs and out on to the lawn to greet the Vicar and Mrs Burder, who was to distribute the prizes. The children were gathered at the starting-point, clutching their collecting baskets and already casting their gazes towards the rockery and the hedges, the outlines of the topiary lost in spring growth, for the gardener had enlisted at the outbreak of war. Miss Darke was consulting her fob-watch. The whistle she had borrowed from Miss Cadogan hung from a silk cord round her neck.

'Now remember,' she said to the children, 'that when you find an egg, lift it carefully. A broken egg does not count. Keep within school bounds. Are you on your marks? Get set! Go.' She blew the whistle and they raced away, with the exception of the Vicar's children who laconically began to search the ground near at hand. Edwin Reed leaned upon his bicycle and smiled.

'Well,' said the Vicar. 'I must be off on Shanks's pony. I have a sermon to write.'

Madame caught sight of Miss Cadogan trudging alone along the lakeside path, then begin the ascent of the incline towards them. 'Please,' she said urgently, 'stay a few moments.' Her voice lowered. 'I need your help. *My ward has vanished.*'

'Vanished?' repeated Mr Burder so loudly that Phyllis and Betty and Millie and Dolly looked at one another and moved just a step or two from their posts in order to hear Madame's reply.

'We have not seen her since early morning. She was not at breakfast, nor in Church.'

'Perhaps she is in her dormitory.'

'We have looked everywhere,' said Madame despairingly. 'Miss Cadogan gave up her luncheon in order to search the grounds. Well, Miss Cadogan,' she called, 'was there any sign?'

Miss Cadogan, breathless, shook her head. She came and stood by them, panting a little, thinking that a game of hockey was less exhausting than the lengthy trudge over uneven ground.

'Swim, does she?' asked the Vicar, and simultaneously all three looked towards the lake.

Madame interlocked her fingers, pressing them together. 'I don't know. I need your advice. What shall we do?'

The Vicar was about to answer when he became aware of Edwin Reed possibly only two feet away. He had crept closer, was certainly within earshot, as the Reverend Burder told his wife that evening. It had been like the game of Grandmother's footsteps. No one had seen him moving, so furtive had been his approach.

'Come along, Edwin,' the Vicar said cheerfully, but with a note of admonition. 'You want to try for a prize, don't you? There won't be any eggs left.'

Edwin smiled, his tongue darted in and out, then he set off, dangling his small collecting basket, a receptacle that looked so sweet in a child's hand and so ludicrous in his. Within seconds he was retrieving eggs from among the spring flowers along the herbaceous border.

'His mother must have sent him up here, poor woman,' said the Vicar.

'Well, I wish she hadn't,' answered Madame sharply, and added, because she could not sound uncharitable before a man of the cloth, 'especially at a time when I feel so distraught.'

'Give her another hour,' said the Vicar. 'I say, give

Madeleine an hour, and if she hasn't put in an appearance by then, make a telephone call to the police station. You have a telephone in the school, do you not?'

Madame nodded. 'It is a necessity.'

'Would you mind if I went in and had a bite to eat?' Miss Cadogan said suddenly. 'I feel positively faint.' Indeed, at that moment, the Vicar's face blurred and his voice sounded far away.

'Please. How thoughtless of me.'

'I ate very little breakfast.'

'I beg of you to go in at once, Miss Cadogan. I insist. And thank you again for your efforts.'

Five minutes later the games mistress was standing at the kitchen table wolfing down her lunch, observed only by Florrie, who wished she had the courage to take a snap.

'She was picking up the food with her fingers,' said Florrie to Betty in the Art Room where they had been sent to fetch the cardboard sign advertising the sale of lemonade. (*Large Glasses one penny, small* – this was written small – *a halfpenny*. Underneath were drawings illustrating both size and coin, and the words *Freshly made, cool and sweet*.)

'I don't believe you,' said Betty. She knew that no member of staff would use such disgusting behaviour and she believed Florrie to be an habitual liar, having caught her out before.

Florrie flushed. There was no point in arguing with a prefect who could report you to Madame. She picked up the sign (it was a rule at Fairwater House that tasks were carried out by two girls even when, as in this instance, it needed only one) and stood aside for Betty to go first downstairs.

It was as they descended that the voices reached them, Madame's first. ' . . . I dare not leave it much longer. . . .' Then Miss Cadogan's, stronger but not altogether audible. '. . . . everywhere . . . no sign . . . I'm afraid.' Madame spoke again. 'I fear for her safety. The Vicar. . . .' and then the churning sound of the telephone handle which connected the speaker to the Fairwater Edge exchange. 'Oh, operator,' the girls heard her say, talking loudly and clearly now in order to be heard over the wires, 'This is Mrs Pennington from the school. Put me through to the police station. It is an emergency.' There was a pause, and then she said, 'I fear some harm has occurred to one of my pupils. I would be grateful if you would send an officer up here at once.'

The two girls stood on the stairs as frozen, Florrie said afterwards to her dormitory companions, as ice-maidens. Down below, in the stairwell where the telephone hung on the wall, they could see the tops of the heads of Madame and Miss Cadogan, and Madame's raised hand as she pressed the ear-pierce against the loop of her hair.

'Thank you,' said Madame. 'I do not wish to lose any more time.' Her last words were indistinct. ('Probably goodbye,' said Betty.) The women walked along the passage to the garden door, paused for a moment, spoke and then went outside. When Betty and Florrie reached the lemonade table, Miss Cadogan had retrieved her neck-cord and whistle from Miss Darke and was ready to call the egg-hunters home, while the Principal was conversing with Mrs Burder in a manner that gave no indication of her turmoil within.

'She's dead,' Florrie whispered to Gertie.

'Quite obviously something dreadful has happened,' Betty confied to Millie.

'Murdered?' asked Millie, agog.

'I think she's run away.' Dolly had joined them. She sounded almost matter of fact.

'But wouldn't she have said something . . . to someone . . .?'

Dolly shook her head. 'She never said a thing about herself. She was secretive.'

'She thought only of others,' said Florrie defensively. 'She was the most unselfish person I've ever know.'

'Stop saying *was*.'

'In fact she's probably half way to France by now.'

'You don't think, do you, that she could be a spy?' They all turned to stare at Gladys. Gertie gasped:

'Of course she's not a spy,' snapped Betty. 'We all know she's the daughter of Madame's cousin.'

'That's just it,' said Gladys. 'They might *all* be in it. They're none of them English.'

Miss Cadogan blew a piercing blast on her whistle, waited and then blew two more.

'Egg counters ready,' called Miss Darke.

'Egg counters,' called Betty to those who had not heard.

From different parts of the grounds the hunters returned to base. The Vicar's children arrived first, hoping to pool their booty, the youngest disgracing them with tears at Miss Cadogan's firm refusal. 'My goodness, I should say not.' As soon as Edwin Reed presented his basket it was clear that no one else would scoop first prize. 'Ten or twelve at least,' murmured Betty, casting her eyes over the pile. 'He's cracked one. Does one count it?'

'Such a pity,' said the Vicar's wife who had been looking forward to presenting the prizes, 'that it couldn't have been won by a child.'

Madame clapped her hands to silence the chattering of the crowd. The egg baskets were all on display now, and a number of people were sipping lemonade.

'Mrs Burder,' Madame announced, 'has very kindly consented to give the prizes this afternoon. With all the onerous duties that befall a Vicar's wife, we are especially grateful to her for giving up her time.'

There was applause as Mrs Burder took her place. 'She wasn't asked, you know,' said Miss Darke to Miss Cadogan. 'Madame approached the Vicar.'

'I am proud,' began Mrs Burder, 'to have been invited to Fairwater House.' (Miss Cadogan smiled at Miss Darke.) 'I think everyone here shares my gratitude to the pupils who have of their own devising so successfully combined patriotic zeal with the traditional jollity I recall from my own childhood.'

In the distance, far away, came the sound of an approaching motor-cycle. The small boys of Fairwater Edge and Fairwater Green became more alert than at any time that afternoon.

'When those brave British prisoners receive the welcome parcels under the auspices of the Red Cross, they will only hazard a guess from whence the chocs, the socks, the tins of precious foods so commonplace to us at home. . . .'

The motor-cycle engine was now sufficiently close to compete with Mrs Burder's voice.

'. . . from whence they came,' she said, a little louder. 'These are dark days of conflict. If I may digress, if you will permit me a moment or two to speak of a subject dear to my heart . . .'

No one heard her. Between the trees edging the drive the motor-cycle flashed in and out of vision, then hurtled, roaring, to a halt, terrifying the Vicar's pony where it was tethered (with its trap) to a post. The Vicar's youngest daughter, who loved it, burst into tears for the second time.

The driver, wearing a leather helmet and goggles, dismounted. In the sidecar sat the local constable, Billy Best, goggles under his helmet. He was a big man, his knees were drawn up and his arms jammed to his sides in the small, egg-shaped cockpit. The driver lifted his goggles and revealed himself to be the senior police officer from Fairwater Green. He released Billy (whose young brothers were on the lawn) and walked purposefully towards Madame, who was hurrying up the slope to meet him.

'I do not think,' went on the Vicar's wife, her voice raised, 'that at any time has the Spirit of Womanhood been more urgently called upon. Young as you are, your contribution on the Home Front is of incalculable value to boys in the trenches.'

'They must have found her,' said Dolly.

'A square knitted for a blanket, pocket money spent on sweetmeats for a dear brother or father or uncle. . . .' intoned the Vicar's wife.

'No,' said Gladys. 'They're not being decisive.' Madame was seen to be talking urgently, the officer was nodding and Billy Best had caught sight of Ida smiling at him through the window.

Mrs Burder at last realized that her audience's attention was elsewhere. Her gaze followed theirs.

'*Please carry on,*' said Miss Darke.

The Vicar's wife grasped the seriousness of the situation. 'An emergency?' Miss Darke confirmed it. Mrs Burder thrilled.

'May I please have your attention,' she commanded. 'I am going to present the prizes.' At the same moment the distant figures of Madame and the two policemen disappeared into the house.

The police officer gazed intently at the two pictures in his hands. One was a sketch portrait from an art class when each girl had drawn her neighbour, the other was a snapshot.

'Is the drawing a good likeness?' he asked Madame, who sat close to her study fire. She found she was trembling uncontrollably although she had managed to remain calm until this moment. He turned the paper round, and she compelled herself to examine it. The hair was right, the cheekbones too, but the eyes were wrong, the proportions distorted although it was difficult to pinpoint exactly where.

'An impression,' she said at last. 'For those of us who know her it is recognizable. But for a stranger, I have my doubts.'

He gave her the snapshot. 'Who took it?'

'One of my pupils, a keen photographer. Her father is a Member of Parliament,' she added, as if to excuse the shadow that cut across Madeleine's face.

'Has she taken others, do you think?'

'I will find out.' She went across to the door and pressed the servant's bell.

'May I have your permission to circulate a description to the Port Authorities, in case she attempts to sail for the Continent?'

Madame put her hand to her throat. 'That is impossible.'

'I regret that it is not. A number of people have managed to board troop-carrying ships . . .'

'Impossible for my ward to do such a thing,' said Madame firmly, although she was stricken with sudden doubts. 'It would be against her background, her nature.'

'In my professional life,' said the police officer gently, 'I have found that human nature is sometimes concealed by outward appearances.'

'Not in this case. I can assure you she would not venture even as far as the next town unchaperoned. In *my profession* I am an expert on the characters of my girls.'

'Murderers,' said the police officer, 'are frequently described by those who knew them as gentle souls.'

'Murderers,' echoed Madame. She needed to sit down, she all but fell into her chair.

'From all you tell me of the young lady she has probably sprained her ankle and is waiting sensibly for a search party to discover and assist her.' The police officer spoke with a comforting calm that did nothing to dispel the principal's gripping terror. 'For that reason, Ma'am, if you will allow me, I should like to organize a search party before dark.'

In the kitchen Billy Best, his helmet on the table, sat drinking tea with pretty Ida and silly Ada and found out what he could.

'What's she like then, this young French lady?' The scullery maids looked at one another and giggled.

'Run off with 'er sweet'eart, 'as she?'

'Oh no!' said Ada. Ida said nothing. Billy looked at her with sharp blue eyes.

'A proper young lady, then? Is that right, Ida Brown?'

Ida smiled. 'How should I know?' She picked up the teapot as the servant's bell rang, the red disc oscillating in the box above the door. 'Go on,' said Ida to Ada. 'You're wanted upstairs.'

Reluctantly, Ada stood.

'How's about another cup?' said Ida to Billy Best.

Florrie, having been fetched from the garden by Ada, told the police officer that she had, indeed, taken a picture of Madeleine that very morning as they set out to conceal the eggs. She enjoyed a feeling of immense importance as she stood in the principal's study and answered the vital questions. Out of the corner of her eye she could see Madame almost collapsed in her chair, as if her strength had run out of her. Florrie and the police officer were the ones in control and Florrie perhaps held the vital clue in her camera.

'Your photograph may give us her direction. From her appearance we may be able to gather whether or not she intended to return. She may be carrying a purse which could contain her passport. You have your headmistress's permission to develop the film immediately.'

'You are excused clearing up duties in the garden,' said Madame in a tone more authoritative than her demeanour suggested.

'I believe you sleep in the same dormitory,' the police officer said as Florrie opened the door. 'I want you to think very hard about Madeleine's behaviour during the last weeks. I need to establish that there was no reason she might have wished to run away.'

Florrie worked in the glow of the red oil lamp. Her little darkroom was warm and stuffy and as she poured the developing fluid into a dish she thought that in a way she was summoning up Madeleine's presence, as a medium might. Madeleine's features would appear, a shadow of the reality, emerging like a ghost. In life Madeleine was vividly colourful, her thick glorious hair full of lights, her irises luminously bright. Florrie would produce a drowning image floating beneath the liquid level, Madeleine without substance, a dead memory, lost in time. Florrie's mind was swimming with her own thoughts, making her dizzy with excitement and fear. She often thought of death and of 'spirits walking abroad', of the energy it took for the departed to penetrate the minds of the living. Last summer, at the end of the holidays, she had met secretly with her cousins late at night. They had crept from their rooms and out into the garden. At midnight they had called upon disembodied souls with the aid of candles and a Bible and a key, and Florrie's cousin Rex had interpreted messages from a Roman soldier and a child who had died walled up during the Jacobean rebellion.

We could do it tonight with Madeleine, thought Florrie. If she is dead she will answer us. She was shaking as she pegged up her photographs to dry.

'We can't,' said Gladys. 'It's wrong.'

'It's *faked*,' said Gertie. 'My parents have been to seances and they said the whole thing is a ruse.'

'How can it be faked if *we're* doing it, you idiot,' said Florrie. 'I tell you, it really works.'

'The dead aren't meant to speak to us, I know they aren't,' whispered Gladys.

'It's electricity then,' Gertie said firmly. 'But if you really want to, Florrie, I'm ready to come along.'

Dolly said nothing, watching their flushed faces as Gladys continued to protest as to the morality of it and Gertie to scorn. Madeleine would scarcely manifest herself for Florrie, clinging, irritating, possessive, bossy Florrie.

'Since you've overheard us,' Florrie said, 'you'd better be in on it.'

Dolly smiled slightly. 'Thank you. I would be most interested to observe.'

The men came equipped with knobkerries, hoes and besom brooms. They came willingly, glad to break the monotony of Sunday, glad to be freed from the evening service. Billy Best, familiar with the grounds, having trespassed there frequently in his childhood, directed them to every part, the copse and the long meadow and the undulating scrubland known locally as Shepherd's Dell. He took for himself the lake path and the caves, lighting a kerosene lamp as dusk fell. Moths flew into its glare or perhaps, thought

Billy, the fan of light merely illuminated a segment of air already thick with flying insects.

The bushes had grown since he was last there, the scrub was thicker. With his stick he held the foliage aside and, stooping, shone his lamp into the first of the caves, remembering how he and his schoolfellows had played truant one winter's day and built a fire there to keep warm. The Major had walked past, his brogue shoes crunching on the sandy path. It was his trysting place, the boys said, with Clara Vernon, the postmistress, who had been a young woman then. Mrs Pennington, of course, knew nothing about it.

The cave was empty. Billy straightened and let the bushes spring back into place, clearing a path for himself to the next. It was empty too, although there were signs of recent occupation, a heap of sacking on the floor. Billy lifted it on his stick, saw patches of mildew and let it fall. Spiders ran from it into the dark recesses. Well, the Major was in his grave and Clara Vernon was a dried old maid. Perhaps it was Ida, although he hoped it wasn't because if Ida was fancy-free he was thinking of walking out with her himself.

His thoughts were on Ida and not Madeleine as he walked back to the stables where the search party had agreed to meet. Under the thick sole of his boot an eggshell crunched. He felt it, turned his lamp on it, saw that it was a relic from the afternoon's hunt and not a nest built in the long grass – he had protected eggs, even as a boy, had never gone nesting – and continued up the slope. From all directions the men were returning, swiping at the undergrowth as they walked, shaking their heads and calling out: 'Not a sign!' 'Nothing nowhere!' and 'No luck at all!'

The senior police officer was hungry and anxious to return home. He had been off duty when the emergency call came and Billy Best had arrived hot-foot from the station. He had been taking a post prandial nap before the arrival of his sister and the delights of his wife's high tea, her potted meat, boiled ham, seedcake and wine jelly. Now the tea would be over, cleared away. Food would have been saved for him but the enjoyment would not be the same. He had been looking forward to a leisurely meal set in the front room, a fire in the grate, the lace cloth on the table and the Sunday tea-service (cream coloured with a pattern of violets) advantageously displayed. Instead of reminiscing with his sister he had been searching the old stables at Fairwater House, clambering into the loft, moving discarded cart and carriage wheels, shafts and tackle in anticipation of discovering a body. He was relieved that his search revealed nothing worse than the remains of a rat caught in a forgotten trap. He had found bodies before, a tramp in a barn and a cat burglar who had slipped from a roof, but this was different. No one had cared about the tramp, and the cat burglar had caused his family fear and misery (as he discovered at the inquest). To have to break the news to Mrs Pennington whom he respected and admired, that the young lady had met with a bad end was an ordeal he had contemplated with a heavy heart. When the men came back from their search of the school grounds he thanked them profoundly and offered them tea and bread and cheese in the school kitchens (as he had been instructed to do) but refrained himself from taking refreshment.

'The lady is at evening service,' he said. 'I will take it upon myself to meet her and break the news to her that we have had no success. First,' he said to Ida, 'I would like to make use of the telephone.'

Matron stood in the doorway of the Pink Dormitory and watched Gertie lift her mattress and conceal the book underneath.

'What are you doing, Gertie?' she asked, and Gertie sprang back and gasped and said, 'I came upstairs to fetch a handkerchief, Matron.'

'I doubt that you keep it beneath your mattress. Please hand me that book.' Her voice grew icy. '*Is it a novel?*'

'It's my Bible.' Gertie withdrew it and placed it in Matron's outstretched hand.

'I hope that you did not intend to read it after Lights Out, Gertie?' Her face, framed in the starched white cap, softened visibly. She almost smiled.

'No, Matron.'

'I do not wish to find you up here again during recreation hour.'

'No, Matron.'

'There is no need,' said Matron standing aside to let Gertie pass, 'no need at all to hide the *Bible*, my dear.'

The Vicar waited to speak to Madame and Miss Darke who came last from the church. 'I shall continue my prayers,' he said. 'God will deliver her safely to you.' It had been a small congregation this evening for a number of men, so he understood, were helping in the search for the missing girl. His congregation was becoming more and more dominated by the fair sex. If it wasn't for the cadets, he thought, it could well be that in another six months there would be no men under forty in either Fairwater Edge or Fairwater Green, save for himself and Doctor Ford who had, poor chap, returned wounded from the front. His wife cherished the romantic hope that the doctor and Major Pennington's widow would stand before the altar. If hostilites had not broken out that hope might have been fulfilled, but now it seemed remote. The war changed everything.

'I will call on you tomorrow,' he told Madame. She pressed her prayer book with gloved fingers, thanked him in a low voice. Miss Darke touched her arm.

'Madame . . . over there!'

The senior police officer was waiting beside his motorcycle. As the two ladies looked in his direction he took a few steps towards them. They met at the church gate.

'I am afraid,' he said, and in this pause Miss Darke put out her hand to give support, 'that we have found no trace of her. It is now necessary to take further steps.'

Each pupil at Fairwater House took a full bath once a

week. The rota, worked out by Matron, was posted in the dormitories. Every night the geyser was lit and first a junior, then a senior girl would, under Matron's supervison, enjoy the luxury of the bathroom that Major Pennington had had installed soon after he had taken possession of the family house.

On this particular evening Florrie had bathed early and Dolly was waiting her turn for the water to become hot. She had just entered the bathroom with her towel and spongebag, when there was a loud knocking on the door, loud and persistent enough to be heard above the sound of the hissing geyser. There was, of course, no key or bolt, for a girl might become ill in the heat and need assistance, and the handle turned before Dolly could reach it to reveal Florrie, flushed and excited, her glasses becoming instantly opaque from the steam.

'Turn off the water, Dolly! We are all wanted downstairs. Madame is going to address us!'

'What about my bath?' Dolly had been looking forward to it, to the solitude it was difficult to achieve at any other time of the week.

'We are all to go down immediately.' Florrie opened the door wider to prove her words, and Dolly saw the smaller girls emerging from their dormitories, already in their night clothes. Matron, at the top of the stairs, lined them up and then led them down.

'Go ahead. I shan't be a few moments.' Dolly turned the taps, wondering if she should remove the plug or whether she would be allowed to return. I'll leave the water, she thought. Whatever it is, it cannot take too long at this hour. She descended to the recreation room where the girls sat in rows of chairs and on the floor. Betty made room for her and Dolly had not even time to sit down before Madame entered and they all rose to their feet. Gladys, who was door monitor, closed it and stood to attention as was the rule.

'Please be seated,' said Madame, and sat on the chair placed ready for her, facing her girls. She waited a moment before she spoke again, and when she did her voice lacked its customary resonanace. 'I have to tell you that the search this afternoon was not successful. I cannot believe that Madeleine has deliberately gone away. I want to ask if any girl has reason to suspect that Madeleine left of her own volition.'

There was silence. One or two girls looked at each other. Then there was a half-hearted chorus. 'No, Madame.'

'Then we have to face, with courage, the possibility that harm has befallen her. It is now twelve hours since she was last seen in the grounds. The police officer in charge of the search has asked the help of our gallant army. Those of you with some scientific knowledge, those of you who have brothers, will be aware that a cannon fired over water will, by breaking the waves of sound, will cause . . .' Her voice faltered, she paused, then continued, '. . . will cause to rise to the surface any object lying on the bed beneath.' She broke off. There was a sob from a girl in her audience, a slight disturbance as her neighbours gave comfort.

'We must all pray for Madeleine tonight,' said Madame, rising. 'Please God tomorrow she will be back with us . . . unharmed.'

Gladys opened the door and pressed herself against it as the headmistress, unable to utter further, swept out.

'Form a line,' called Miss Darke. 'It is time for bed.'

'Dolly, you will have to forgo your bath,' said Matron. 'Lights out in fifteen minutes.'

'Don't forget,' whispered Gertie, pressing her arm surreptitiously as she passed.

At the Royal Field Artillery Barracks some six and a half miles away, six soldiers were attaching a gun to a limber and the limber to a team of six horses. Six was an important number, said Florrie, as the six girls crowded into her little darkroom. The total must be divisble by three.

'How are we going to *breathe?*' asked Gladys, frightened already.

'Shut the door,' said Florrie. As she spoke, she lit the oil

41

lamp and replaced the red funnel. Her black shadow lengthened up the wall, and all their faces seemed suffused with blood.

'I don't want to stay,' whispered Gladys.

'You have to,' said Millie. 'You heard what Florrie said. There has to be six of us.'

'Gertie! The Bible.'

Dora put it in Florrie's red hands.

'I really want to go,' said Gladys.

'Who has the ribbon?'

Dolly put her hand into her dressing-gown pocket and brought out her hair-ribbon. 'Matron's on the prowl,' she said. 'I had to go into hiding by the hall cupboard.'

'What *happened?*'

'She came out of her room just as I closed the dormitory door. Then she went into the WC!'

They began to giggle, Gladys more hysterically than the rest.

'Then I shot along here. I heard her flush the cistern just as I arrived!'

'Lock the door,' ordered Florrie. 'I want to start.' Gertie, closest to it, turned the key.

'Give it to me.'

'Oh don't lock the door,' begged Gladys. 'Suppose the lamp caught fire . . .'

Florrie took the key and threaded Dolly's hair-ribbon through it. 'You have to put the key in at the Seventh Psalm.'

'God won't like it,' said Gladys. 'I think we should stop.'

'The psalm makes it safe, silly,' said Phyllis. 'Otherwise it would be devil's work. That's right, isn't it, Florrie?'

Florrie put the Bible on the table, the key protruding, the dark blue ribbon looking black under the light. She opened the little cupboard under the sink and took out a photograph of Madeleine. 'I didn't show them this one. I took it last year.'

'Not her photograph . . .' moaned Gladys. The others

crowded round Florrie, the image of Madeleine seeming both to excite and repel.

Gertie drew back. 'It's not a good likeness.'

'She had no idea I was taking it. She never let me.'

'I'm not surprised,' said Dolly with a slight smile, 'Judging by the results.'

'The light was wrong,' answered Florrie. She placed the picture on the floor. 'We have to form a circle now.'

They drew back a little. 'I'm going to stand in the middle. Hold hands.'

She suspended the Bible by the ribbon attached to the key. A loop was wound round the leather binding, holding the pages firm, the key in place. 'If it swings to the right it means yes. To the left, no.'

The Bible hung there, unmoving.

'We have to see if anyone is there,' said Florrie. 'I'm going to try now.' She spoke in an artificial voice. 'Is anyone there?' They stood, gripping one another's hands, breathless. 'Everyone think of Madeleine. Madeleine. Madeleine. Is anyone there?'

The Bible suddenly swung a little and revolved to the right.

'Will you help us,' intoned Florrie, 'to find Madeleine Maurel?'

The Bible swung to the right.

'Who is it?' gasped Gertie.

'Are you the spirit of a child?' It swung to the left. 'Of a lady long dead?' It went to the left again. 'Are you the spirit of a gentleman?' This time the circumlocution was to the right. Gladys gave a little moan.

Gertie urged, 'Find out when he died.'

'Did you pass on during the nineteenth century?' It circled right. 'Were you British?' Right again. 'Were you forefather to one of us here?' The Bible turned so fast the ribbon twisted. Gladys began to cry. 'To me?' asked Florrie in the dreadful voice. No. 'To Dolly?' No again. Gladys was crying uncontrollably, trying to free herself from the restraining hands either side of her. Phyllis and Gertie held fast.

'To Gertie?' asked Florrie. The Bible went to the left. 'To Gladys?'

Gladys began to shriek. 'Open the door. I'm going to die.' .

'You're perfectly safe.'

'There's plenty of air.'

'Open the door! Open the door!' Gladys broke free, hurled herself against it and began to hammer it. They tried to pull her away. Unaccountably to herself, Millie began to cry as well. A violent knocking from the other side echoed Gladys's pounding fists.

'Open the door at once. Whoever is in there, open the door *immediately!*'

Florrie struggled with the knot tying the Bible.

Madame's voice commanded, 'Open the door.'

Doldy snatched the Bible from Florrie, forced the pages open, tore out the key and put it in the lock. There was one frozen second which remained in the minds of all of them ever afterwards, the broken circle of terrified faces, red from the lamp, then Dolly turned the key and the door was thrust instantly open and Madame and Matron faced them, livid with anxiety and rage.

Gladys flung herself at them, sobbing and screaming.

Matron said, 'All of you, go back to your dormitories at once.'

They filed past her, one by one, ashamed and silent. Matron bent to lift Gladys to her feet, picked up the photograph of Madeleine and handed it to Madame.

'I know she's dead,' wept Gladys. 'I'm frightened of her spirit.'

The outrider, an artillery officer, turned into the school drive. After him, between the hedgerows, came the six horses, a bombardier astride the leader. Six men were riding on the limber with the gun. They jumped off at their officer's command, manhandling the gun from its holdings and manoeuvring it down the slope towards the lake. The officer secured the horses, the bombardier held up a storm lantern to facilitate his men, although the moon was up.

From the upper windows of the school the pale faces of the girls from the Green Dormitory looked out; Matron pulled aside the curtains of the sick room where Gladys now slept exhausted, and watched the soldiers struggling to run the cannon over the uneven ground. In the scullery Constable Billy Best said to Ida, 'Come on, I'll walk you back home.' In her study, Madame Pennington put a shawl round her shoulders and sat down beside the dead fire. She recalled the day with a sense of disbelief. The Easter Egg Hunt, in prospect, promised to be a happy occasion.

Doctor Ford entered without knocking. He looked drawn, his complexion greyish white.

'You must put a stop to amateur photography,' he said severely. 'The girl who was responsible for the dangerous occult nonsense must be sent home. You must not keep her in the school.'

Madame turned up the flame of the lamp beside her. 'Gladys? Is she in a better state of mind?'

'I had to assure her she was not possessed by the devil. She's asleep now. Matron is with her.' His voice grew angry. 'You know what they were up to, I suppose?'

Madame nodded and stretched out her hand to him. 'Robert, what in God's name am I going to do?'

He took her hand, and still holding it sat down facing her. 'Rest. When did you last take something to eat or drink?'

'They think she has drowned. They are going to fire a cannon across the lake.'

'I know.'

She looked into his eyes. 'Why did you say she was not ill?'

He took his hand away, stood, walked to the window, then turned and confronted her. 'There was nothing wrong with her.'

'I respect your opinion . . . of course . . . but if, in spite of all outward appearances . . . she may have fallen, unconscious.'

'Her symptoms were in her mind. All in her mind.'

For a moment she covered her face with her hands. 'I cannot describe the horrors in my brain.'

'I shall instruct Matron to heat some milk for you to take before you sleep.'

'Do you imagine I will sleep?'

Doctor Ford picked up the sketch of Madeleine which still lay on the piano and contemplated it. He made no reply. He seemed lost to her. She said at last, 'It does not resemble her.'

He started and put down the picture.

'You look exhausted too,' said Madame Pennington. 'Thank you for coming. I am so grateful for your presence.'

'You have searched everywhere? The school? The grounds?'

'Everywhere . . . except. . . .' she gestured towards the window and the remainder of her words was obliterated by the boom of the cannon. She leapt to her feet, and Doctor Ford put his arm round her shoulders to comfort her. The reverberations seemed to go on for a long time.

In the dormitory Dolly, Gertie and Florrie lay awake long after the noise had died away. By the moonlight Madeleine's empty bed looked white and flat, the cover pulled up like a shroud.

At the lakeside the soldiers put their shoulders to the wheel as they manhandled the gun up the steep slope towards the waiting horses. The explosion had caused waves on the usually still water. The police officer and the bombardier waited and watched until dead fishes rose with the dawn, but there was no sign of the missing girl. Madame thanked God that her ward had not drowned and daily expected some news, gradually becoming reconciled to the idea that for some reason she had left of her own free will.

No news came. As the months passed so expectation dwindled although hope never died and the girls talked of her from time to time.

But the mystery remains unsolved.
Madeleine did not return. She was never found.

Part Two

Madeleine's Story

The Editor
An Argosy of Mystery Tales
Magazine House
Fleet Street
London   14 June 1926

Dear Sir,

Some years ago you published a short story of mine called 'A Strange Disappearance.' Many of your contributions begin with the words 'this is a true story' when patently they are not. Mine was a genuine account with only one (deliberate) falsehood. The author was referred to as being of the masculine gender.

At the time I knew more than I dared to write, and since then, by dint of questioning and following 'leads' I have learned more. I am now married and live in the vicinity where the events I described took place. I am hoping that the enclosed manuscript will be of interest to you. Possibly you could publish it together with the earlier version.

Yours faithfully
(signed) A. Oxford

Mrs A. Oxford
Hill Cottage
East Mere
Rutland

Dear Madam

Thank you for sending us 'Madeleine's Story' which we have read with great interest. Unfortunately, however, we are unable to use it for publication, since its length exceeds our specified limit. We also feel that the subject matter is unsuitable for a magazine of this kind.

Yours faithfully
(signed) William MacMillan
Editor

I have to go back to the beginning, to Madeleine's arrival at Fairwater House School where I was already a pupil. I do not intend to identify myself further. Suffice it to say that I was sufficiently established there before the outbreak of war to be struck by the changes that inevitably took place, although Madame Pennington did her utmost to resist them. From this the reader will deduce I am not the girl I have called Florrie, but there will be no further clues. Unlike Oswald, E. Nesbit's 'author' of *The Treasure Seekers*, I will not reveal myself inadvertently. I remember so well our secret hoard of novels, brought back after the holidays – our reading matter was strictly supervised by Miss Darke – and that our Nesbit craze was at its height the term that Madeleine joined us. Fires were never lit in the dormitories and we concealed the contraband fiction above the bird traps sealing the chimneys. Rider Haggard, Angela Brazil, Charlotte Brontë, Louisa Alcott, Susan Coolidge lay stacked upon those metal trays above the grates, all forbidden. What would we do, we wondered, if a bird actually fell and beat against the chimney walls. Fortunately it never happened. Madeleine, perhaps because she herself had need of a hiding place, discovered Gertie's library and being mid-way between pupil and teacher it was feared she would report the breach of rules. Gertie, a sophisticated reader, had a volume by Elinor Glyn. Madeleine, however, said nothing – beyond asking Gertie if she might borrow the book!

It is difficult not to digress. I will now effect my own concealment with as much care as we lodged our books behind the chimney breasts. I will disappear into the third person narrative.

'Look!' said Gertie, pointing upwards. The group of girls at the window had been watching the drive, but now they turned their concerted gaze towards the sky. On that cloud-less September afternoon the plane soared above the hockey field (or so it seemed) and dropped vertically, only to soar again and veer from view.

'Which one is it, do you think?' asked Phyllis.

'Oh the handsome one with blue eyes.' Betty grasped her arm. 'He's coming back now. I believe he's going to loop the loop.'

'It must be the trainer, then,' said Dolly. 'The cadets wouldn't be allowed to do tricks like that.'

'Who says, Miss Know-all!'

'My Uncle is in the Flying Corps.'

'You've never said so before.'

'There was no reason.'

High over the lake now the plane climbed into the sky, the big round target markings on each wing tip making it look like some giant moth. The sun caught the surface of the wings and gave the dark green camouflage a sudden patina of silver. As it reached the summit of its curve it seemed to hang in the air, then roll into its descending arc.

At that same moment the car bearing Madeleine and her mother turned into the school gates and Doctor Ford let himself out of the front door and strode towards his horse. For half a minute, perhaps, the noise of the plane and the car merged and Millie, whose hearing was acute, put her hands to her ears. Then the plane flew overhead and out of sight, the car drew up before the house and there was only the diminishing sound of hoofs upon gravel.

Madame Pennington heard the engine of the car, heard the jangle of the door bell. It was many years since she had seen her cousin and although she had been excited all morning at the reunion, now the moment was approaching she was gripped by panic. These wretched nerves, she said to herself, and wished that Doctor Ford had stayed a few minutes longer. His mere presence calmed her. I am upset, she thought, because Vera has given notice and the other servants might follow suit. Vera's footsteps in the hall below had a new defiance, just as her voice had done earlier, a triumphant *timbre*, a harsh disinterest. 'My mam thought going in to service was the best possible a girl could aim for. Waiting on my betters. When I came to you first, *Mrs*

Pennington, I wasn't no older than some of your girls here. I'm offering myself for munitions, or canteens. I want to help my country.'

'I need you here, Vera. Indeed, I don't know how I will manage without you.' The blandishments were of no avail.

'You'll have to manage, like everyone else. I dare say Cook will stay, and Ida's too young to be taken. Ada's not bright enough,' she added, 'and perhaps the young ladies could learn to do more for themselves.'

The front door opened and closed, and Madame heard Vera's greeting, her tone more deferential from the years of training. 'Good afternoon, Madam. Good afternoon, Miss.' There was a pause while the visitors divested themselves of their coats, then a murmur and the ascending feet on the stairs. Will she think I've aged, thought Madame Pennington and as Vera knocked, she took a step towards the door.

It was her cousin who had aged, become coarse featured and stout. The two women embraced and Madama Maurel's hat was dislodged. She fussed with the pins, tears in her eyes, laughing a little at the same time.

'Oh my stupid hat! My hair too! You look so young I feel ashamed. It's like a dream, seeing you again.' Madame Pennington reverted to her natural language as though she hadn't been speaking English for well over a decade. 'You're not to worry,' she said. 'I'm going to take her, I don't want a penny . . .'

She looked towards Madeleine who stood not far from the door. The girl was smiling but clearly embarrassed.

'I am prepared to go back to France. Please do not feel constrained.'

Madame took both her hands in welcome. 'I would do it for your mother's sake alone. But you are also the answer to a prayer.' (She couldn't, of course, expect her to take on a parlour maid's duties, but Miss Darke had spoken – in the most casual way – or her training as a VAD and another pair of hands for the duration . . .)

'I want to hear *everything*,' Madame Maurel was saying

excitedly, throwing herself down on to the couch with such vigour her feet left the floor. 'I want to know about your marriage, about the inheritance.'

'This building is the inheritance,' said Madame.

'But I heard you lived with servants in a mansion.'

'Madeleine,' said Madame Pennington, 'You must be anxious to see round your new home. I will find someone to escort you.' She went on to the landing and leaned over the banisters to where she could see the girls lining up below. 'Betty,' she called. 'Please come upstairs for a moment.' She came back into the study, where her cousin had risen from the couch to fuss again with her hat before the glass. 'Madeleine,' said Madame. 'Betty will be your guide. She is one of our senior prefects.'

When the two girls had gone, she snapped at her cousin, 'Now do stop adjusting that wretched hat, Danielle. Sit down. I'll ring for coffee.'

'The only news we ever heard of you was from Aunt Clare. Your mother wouldn't mention your name. We never even saw the wedding photographs.'

Madame Pennington twisted her wedding ring. 'There were no wedding photographs.'

Madame Maurel sat down again heavily. 'It never even *occurred* to me . . .'

'Why should it. You were always a traditionalist.'

'I'm a *romantic*,' Madame Maurel defended herself. 'When you ran away. . . .'

'You assumed I was running away to be married. Now you understand about my "inheritance".'

'He loved you very much.'

'And I him. Anyway, you have no reason to be envious. Henri adored you and he was very handsome.'

'He still is,' said Madame Maurel. 'Perhaps I should say *distinguished* nowadays.' Her eyes filled with tears. 'The war is terrible, Marie. We've heard nothing from him. Nothing. He was delighted to be able to fight again, of course . . . at those moments men do not think of their wives. I wrote to you in desperation. Madeleine. . . .'

'I will take care of Madeleine as if she were my own daughter. You would be welcome to stay too.'

'No, I must go home. My mother needs me. And at any time Henri may return.' She leaned forward. 'You may not have a fortune, but you are an attractive widow. Who was the gentleman I saw riding down the drive?'

Standing beside her mother's cousin, Madeleine waved her handkerchief although, curiously, there were no tears in her eyes. She had imagined that parting from her mother would be excruciatingly painful but as she watched the grey, chauffeur-driven tourer disappear round the bend of the drive, she felt a kind of relief which was totally unexpected. Her mother's cousin – what should she call her? Cousin Marie? Aunt? – put out a reassuring hand, pressed Madeleine's fore-arm. As a matter of fact Madame Pennington experienced a wave of maternal emotion, an overpowering kinship, because she saw in this tall, beautiful young girl a reflection of herself. There was no doubt that Madeleine resembled her more than she did her mother. She is like my grandmother, thought Madame Pennington, she has followed that line, whereas Danielle took everything from her father's side, the peasant forebears!

'Come,' she said, 'we will walk a little, and talk. I am sure it will not be long before you receive a letter from your mother.'

They strolled along the path leading to the vegetable garden. On either side was a border, edged with ageratum and sweet Williams. 'It is very pretty along here in early summer,' said Madame Pennington, 'very colourful when all the flowers are out.' Their conversation lapsed from English into French and back again. 'Because you are a little older your position will not exactly be that of a pupil. Although I cannot treat you as staff.'

'Between the two,' suggested Madeleine. 'Like Jane Eyre.'

'I hope you will be happier.' The principal lowered her voice although there was no one there but the two of them.

'Many parents who would have sent their daughters to finishing school in Switzerland were it not for the hostilities, have turned to us. Because I am French, a knowledge of the language has always been an important part of the curriculum.'

'The war is benefiting the school, Tante.'

'It seems dreadful to say such a thing . . . oh, and Madeleine, I think you should address me as Madame, except when we are alone. My private feelings,' she put her arm around the girl's narrow shoulders, 'will never be formal. Your parents and I, when we were your age, were very close.'

'My mother has always talked about you, about your secret marriage.'

Madame Pennington withdrew her arm. 'You will sleep in a dormitory, of course, but I am placing you with girls I consider congenial companions.'

'The uniform, Madame?' Madeleine tried to control the distaste she had at the idea of wearing such drab attire.

'I cannot make an exception there. One of our senior girls left the school – the clothes will fit you with very little alteration. But if you are acting as chaperon, accompanying the girls on a shopping expedition or to church, then you may wear your own dresses.' Madame plucked the dead head from a chrysanthemum that had straggled over the path. 'I think the additional advantage of French conversation might attract parents of a higher social standing.' She stopped to make the impact greater. 'My dream, Madeleine, is to have one, just one, daughter from the lower realms of the upper classes. I am hoping that this terrible war might bring an end to private education in the home.'

Edwin Reed approached so silently, appeared so instantly before them that Madeleine gasped aloud. He stood on the path before them leaning on his bicycle, as if he had materialized from the air. His hands seemed to be stitched to his sleeves, like a rag doll's. One rested limply on the saddle, the other on the white cloth that covered the handle-basket.

'Edwin!' said Madame, startled too. 'You gave me quite a shock, standing there. Which way did you come?'

He began to talk incomprehensibly, his tongue slipping in and out over his lips. Once a trail of spittle ran down the line from the left side of his mouth to his chin, like a stream breaking its banks and following a dry tributary. Madeleine, still chilled from the encounter, tried to follow his words.

'I cannot understand him, he speaks so fast.'

'My dear,' said Madame Pennington in French, 'no one can. He has no palate.'

Edwin smiled at them – his eye teeth were a brownish-grey – and lifted the cloth from the basket revealing a fine bunch of purple grapes and six peaches. His eyes were fixed on Madeleine, unblinking, as if waiting for her reaction. She hurriedly looked down, then touched a peach.

'They look delicious.'

'Please take them to the kitchen door, Edwin. And thank your mother for me. I will send a note.'

Madame Pennington drew Madeleine on, and Madeleine was compelled to turn her head back to see if he had moved away. He was watching her, and as their eyes met he said something and laughed.

'Poor creature,' said Madame Pennington. 'Don't look at him, Madeleine, or he'll never go.'

'Who is he?'

Madame slipped her arm through Madeleine's. 'His mother is well-to-do, of very good family. Titled. Both through marriage and in her own right. She is Lady Reed. From time to time she sends me fruit grown in her conservatory.'

Madeleine said with a touch of irony lost on her new-found relative, 'Are there no daughters?'

'Alas, no.' As they turned into the walled vegetable garden Edwin again crossed the path in front of them and Madeleine shuddered. 'Don't be afraid of him,' said Madame. 'He always appears when one least expects him, but he is quite harmless.'

'He must have run round the wall and come in through the gate,' said Madeleine horrified.

'What is more, he has delivered the fruit to Cook,' answered Madame Pennington. 'Goodbye, Edwin,' she called. 'You must go home now.'

Obediently he turned and wheeled his bicycle out of the vegetable garden, mounted, and rattled from view.

Madeleine's presence in the school was a source of rivalry and emotional excitement. Her superiority of age, her French clothes ('infinitely more elegant than *anything* one can buy in London'), her accent and her undisputed good looks caused envy and admiration. Her dormitory companions were voted 'lucky dogs' by all and were pestered for details of her conversation, her undergarments, her nightclothes and how she looked when she was asleep. 'Beautiful!' said Gertie.

Madame gave her three weeks to settle in and settle down and then announced the introduction of privileges. 'Now we have Madeleine as chaperon I intend to allow small groups of older girls to shop in the village without a mistress as escort. I will also allow the prefects to walk to church at their own pace.' She had, of course, written to the parents for permission beforehand.

The newly acquired freedom was somewhat curtailed when put into practice. When Betty, Gertie, Phyllis, Dolly, Millie and Madeleine set off for church on the first Sunday they learned that they were to walk in crocodile and that only Madeleine was permitted to wear her 'mufti' coat.

'I do not want you to linger or gossip,' instructed Madame Pennington, straightening Dolly's shoulders and Gertie's hat. 'You will arrive at the village ahead of us. I do not expect to overtake you with the rest of the school.'

'We must make a good start,' Phyllis said, as soon as they were out of earshot, 'because if anything goes wrong we won't be allowed to walk alone again.' At the church gates they were presented with a dilemma. Should they go in and take their places, or should they wait?

59

'We'd better wait,' said Millie. 'We don't want to get told off.'

'Hmm hmm,' went Gertie, making an artificial cough, and rolled her eyes to the right to indicate that Doctor Ford was crossing the Green.

'Do you think he's dashing, Madeleine?' asked Betty. 'You know he's Madame's beau.'

Madeleine raised her eyes as Doctor Ford passed and appraised him in this new light. He nodded, raised his hat and went into the church.

'Are you sure he's her beau?'

'Well, he *may* not be. But he calls quite often.'

'He was a friend of Madame's husband. That's what *she* says, anyway. He's a doctor.'

'Does he listen to her heart, do you think?' asked Gertie with a giggle.

'He listened to *mine*,' boasted Millie, 'when I had measles.'

'Through your chemise, I hope,' said Gertie, then put her hand over her mouth because she saw that Madame was turning from the lane at the head of the school. She smiled at the prefects, and walked swiftly by them. They exchanged glances, glad that they had had the good sense to wait.

The hymn that morning was number 489. 'God moves in Mysterious Ways,' announced the Reverend Burder. The congregation stood and several throats were cleared. The pews were full, the cadets from the training school were in strong voice and young Frederick Palmer, Ada's brother, sang out in a lusty baritone. He was in high spirits because next Sunday he would be part of a garrison and on the way to win the war. His parents sat on either side of him and Gertie noticed that his mother was crying, but whether from pride or sadness it was impossible to tell.

Doctor Ford sang loudly, too, standing square, throwing back his head on the Amen. He was sitting in a forward pew this morning, ahead of the school and Madame, and Madeleine looked once or twice to see if the principal was concentrating upon the hymn, or whether she could not refrain from glancing at her supposed beau. The cadets were certainly aware of the Fairwater girls, they certainly *glanced*, at each other and across the aisle at 'the fair damsels' as Miss Darke sometimes referred to them in her poetic way. Cadet William Kent, known to his friends and family as Will, watched Gertie furtively pencil a note and slip it between the pages of Millie's hymn book, saw Millie read it and stifle her giggles, observed her pass it on to Phyllis who, in turn, passed it to Madeleine who, without looking at it, crumpled it and tucked it in her glove.

Is she a mistress, wondered Will, or a prefect? 'Judge not the Lord by feeble sense,' he sang in his pleasant tenor, his eyes turned in her direction, 'But trust him for his grace.' She wasn't in uniform, yet the girl next to her had not hesitated to pass the note. 'Behind a frowning providence He hides a smiling face.' She hadn't been there when the term began, he would have picked her out immediately. The new cadets had arrived during the summer holidays, had thought it a dreadful dull place to be until that Sunday when the tall, handsome woman who had hitherto sat alone in her pew led in 'a wondrous crocodile' which he had promptly immortalized in verse.

> Oh see the wondrous crocodile
> Which comes not from the distant Nile.
> No snapping jaws
> But rosy lips
> No stunted joints
> But slender hips,
> Flashing orbs
> Silken tresses
> Maidens these
> In Sunday Dresses.
> Fear not th'approaching crocodile
> Danger only in its smile.

('Not particularly good,' said Will's friend, Nigel Jessop, but when challenged could compose nothing better.)

Will did not take Communion. The Vicar passed along

the line of communicants kneeling before the altar rail, placing a wafer on Lady Reed's extended tongue and deciding not to battle with the portcullis of Edwin's clenched teeth. He rather liked the metaphor, reflected on the perversity of the voracious Edwin refusing his morsel when he consumed every cake and biscuit and scone put before him at the Vicarage teas.

'The Body of our Lord Jesus Christ, which was given for thee, preserve thy body and soul unto everlasting life.'

From between his fingers, Will watched Madame move forward to the altar, then his Colonel, the two mistresses who always shared a hymn-book and a number of girls. The one who had taken the note took her place behind the others, and as she went forward slowly Will saw the crushed piece of paper fall from its concealed place in her glove and disappear under the boot of the elderly man behind her. In an instant, Will slipped out of the pew and purloined it. Madeleine, kneeling at the altar, was unaware of her loss. She bowed her head low and Will, the means of introduction now in his hand, was stirred by the sight of a tendril of hair which had escaped from the confines of her hat and lay across the nape of her neck.

'Take and eat this in remembrance that Christ died for thee, and feed on him in thy heart by faith and thanksgiving,' recited the Reverend Burder, dreaming of the fine rib of beef roasting in the oven for his lunch.

Will found no means of approaching his Goddess. (Goddess at the altar rail/Creamy skin, translucent pale.' He intended to finish it later and bring in the recalcitrant curl.) The crocodile had already formed before the cadets left the church. To frustrate him further, the Vicar blocked the doorway as he spoke to a young man who was obviously about to join a regiment.

'I never thought,' the young man was saying, in his soft local accent, 'I'd have the good fortune to see France, Sir.'

'We sang about that this morning, didn't we, Palmer? God moves in mysterious ways.'

'Excuse me, Vicar,' said the Colonel. The Reverend

Burder smiled, pressed Frederick Palmer's shoulder in a fatherly way, and moved aside.

The Fairwater girls turned from sight, and Will put the missive into his pocket.

Each morning, even on those occasions when he had been up all night delivering a baby or attending a dying man, Robert Ford would ride his mare, Sally, across the fields and along the lanes. It was, he always told his patients, more invigorating and refreshing to him than a night's sleep.

On a particularly misty autumn morning, he was out with the first labourers, and already the stubble was burning on the harvested fields, sending wisps of black smoke into the air. Social changes were slow to reach Fairwater. Further South there was little left of the last century, but here the very old still wore gaiters and belted smocks, pattens on their feet in the fields and farm yards, and when the storms were hard the men covered their heads with split sacks. Robert's grandfather had been a gentleman farmer but had sold his land when his only son had become a doctor. Because of it Robert felt a kinship with the workers he would meet on his morning rides, part of him wishing that his father had not taken up medicine or urged him to do so, too.

'Morning, Jim.'

'Morning, Doctor Ford.'

These rural folk liked and trusted him, thought him a little to pernickity about his dress – London fashion some of them called it – and wished he would find himself a wife now that both his parents were gone. Lottie was an excellent housekeeper, but a man needed more than that.

Robert rode past the aerodrome which had once grown maize and wheat. The cadets were on parade, and the outlines of the planes were emerging from the ground mist. The commands of the Warrant Officer rang out into the dawn air. I'd rather hear cows, thought Robert.

He trotted back along the lane admiring, as he always

did at this time of year, the autumn crocuses and overblown roses in the cottage gardens. He relished the idea of tradition, of flora rooted back into the centuries, flourishing in Wordsworth's time and Shakespeare's time. The red lamp, signifying his profession, still burned over his front door. He dismounted, let Sally find her own way along the stable drive, and turned down the light. He called into the 'speaking tube' which his father had installed beside the night bell: 'Lottie, I'm as hungry as a horse. Five minutes and I'll be in.' Then he followed Sally into the yard where her head was already in a trough.

The kitchen door was in two halves, like a stable door itself. It opened directly into the flagged scullery, where Lottie waited with her news.

'There's no peace for the wicked, Doctor. Old Henry's in the surgery. Cut his thumb half off with the meat chopper.'

'I hope we don't find it in our sausages,' said Robert, casting a look at his breakfast sizzling in the pan. He went to the sink and washed his hands under the tap, dried them on a towel suspended from a wooden roller on the door and went through the narrow passage separating the kitchen from the surgery which had been his father's before him.

Henry, the butcher, sat in a bloody apron, his thumb wrapped round with strips of stained linen sheet.

'The missus wrapped it for un, Doctor.'

'Too much porter at the Swan last night,' said Robert. 'You couldn't keep a steady knife.' He began to unwrap the linen.

'It was that blasted sow. She gave me nowt but trouble when she was living, and she's still plaguing me now she's dead.'

Robert looked at the partially severed thumb. 'I'm going to have to sew it for you, Henry.' He went to the mahogany cabinet and opened it, displaying bottles of Lottie's home-made wines; elderberry, elderflower, dandelion and plum. 'What's it to be?'

'Well, plum'd go down nicely,' said Henry, 'though your father always recommended the elderberry for stitches.'

'If it's too painful I can always give you a whiff of ether.'

'And miss my breakfast. No thank you, young man. I had ether once. I was as dizzy afterwards as if I'd been dancing round a maypole.'

The doctor gave the plum wine two minutes to dull the finer reactions and then he took his needle. Even when there was a loud knock at the front door his hand remained steady. Henry sat still as rock.

'You got visitors,' said Henry. 'Or maybe old Jim Wharton's sliced himself with his scythe. I told him he's getting past it.'

In the kitchen Lottie, unhurried, slid the sausages on to an enamel plate, covered it with another and left it on the stove to keep warm. Then she walked – but not briskly – along the whitewashed passage, past the surgery door, through the main living room and opened the front door. The postmistress, Clara Vernon, thrust a telegram into her hand.

'It's for the Doctor. From London.'

'Not bad news from his sister?'

'No. It's official. From the War Office. Though I can't make head nor tail of it.'

'That's a change for you, Clara,' said Lottie. 'Something up and you not the first to know about it.' She took the envelope, made a remark about the weather and closed the door.

A few days after the prefects had been allowed to walk with Madeleine to church, Madame Pennington informed Betty, Dolly and Phyllis that she considered they were sufficiently sensible and trustworthy to go into the village of Fairwater Green and make some small purchases for themselves and for one or two other girls. Gertie needed hair-ribbons, Gladys some Gentian Violet to apply to an ulcer in her mouth, Millie some assorted sweets to offer on her birthday. Early mist had promised a clear day, but by mid-afternoon, as they were on the point of setting out, the sky became grey and a light drizzle began to fall.

'I think perhaps we should postpone the outing,' said Madame, a note of relief apparent in her tone.

The three prefects cast looks of despair at Madeleine.

'We will wear galoshes,' she said, 'and take umbrellas. We would all be disappointed if you cancelled permission now.'

'I would never forgive myself if you caught chills.' Already Madame regretted her leniency in suggesting the trip. It had seemed such a good idea, character forming, in keeping with the times. *I feel*, she had written to the selected parents, *that young women of today should be encouraged, within the bounds of protection, to use their initiative with greater freedom.* But since the parents had replied, all but two being in agreement, Madame had been beset by fears and dreams in which one or another of her charges met with disastrous fate.

'It's easing off, Madame,' Betty ventured. 'The rain has almost stopped.'

'If it is bad,' Madeleine promised, 'we will take shelter. I have the list.' And she held out the paper on which she had written down the requests, as if that in itself made it imperative they should go.

'Very well,' said Madame reluctantly. 'But should anything prevent you from returning by five, please go into the post office and ask Miss Vernon to telephone me.'

Still under her apprehensive eye, the four girls pulled on their galoshes and lined up, two by two, by the door.

'Remember,' said Madame, 'that you represent the school. On no account are you to run or break rank until you reach the village. Use decorum when you are in the shops.'

Madeleine and Betty were the pair in front.

'You've changed our lives, you know,' said Dolly, touching Madeleine's arm. 'We feel human again.'

'Always stuck with juniors or with one of the mistresses to chaperon us. I simply never dared to buy the things I really wanted,' added Betty. 'I would have died if Madame had decided we couldn't go after all.

Fairwater Edge boasted only one small general store, but Fairwater Green, to where the four girls were now bound, was the commercial centre of the surrounding communities. Henry Brown raised his own meat for the Family Butcher's establishment, the shop set back in a garden (it had been in his family since the eighteenth century) with rambler roses growing round the window. On that afternoon a pig's head had pride of place upon the slab, the offending beast whose intransigent limbs had caused the accident to Henry's thumb earlier in the day. Unskinned hares with glazed eyes and legs of mutton hung from hooks, making Dolly more determined than ever to be a vegetarian like George Bernard Shaw just as soon as she was able to determine her own diet.

Across the lane was the bakery and bakehouse, the smithy alongside. Baker and smith were brothers, 'closer than Siamese twins' Lottie (their sister) averred. Miss Vernon's post office was at the front of her cottage. Post-office, Newsagent and Tobacconist, it said over the small window. In the cottage next door lived the dressmaker, a widow, who had a hand-painted sign in front of her living-room curtains, as if everyone from miles around did not know her identity or what she did. Past Doctor Ford's surgery was the Multiple Grocers, Jackson's by name, which caused one affluent parent visiting her daughter to exclaim, 'You see, even in the heart of the country, one need not be cut off from fine foods.' 'Alas,' said Madame, 'it has no connection with your famous London store.'

It was to Jackson's that the girls went first. There was an excellent confectionary counter, and they had commissions for others besides Millie's official order. Gertie had asked for toffee pieces, others for pear drops and peppermints and licorice laces. While Phyllis was overseeing the weighing, making certain that each ounce was in a separate bag, Madeleine went across to the Toiletries and Pharmaceuticals, where Miss Jackson presided.

'I would like some papier poudre.'

Betty joined her. 'You don't *wear* it, do you?' Madeleine smiled and slipped it in her purse.

'Is that why your skin looks so blissfully smooth? I'm going to buy some too.'

'All right,' said Madeleine, 'but if you're caught don't say that you had the idea from me.'

As they came out into the lane, Dolly announced, 'I'm going to post a letter.'

'You can't!' said Phyllis. 'Suppose you're seen?'

'I don't want this one read by Madame,' said Dolly defiantly. 'Keep *cave* for me.' She walked boldly across the road and in through the post office door.

The Doctor was standing by the counter, but before Dolly could go out again, Miss Vernon emerged from the room at the back with a flat cigarette box.

'I made them up mild, Doctor.' She handed them across the counter. As he took them, was about to speak, the warning bell rang on the telegraph instrument.

'Telegrammes all morning,' said Miss Vernon. 'And my girl poorly. It's hard to get on.'

'I'm afraid I was responsible for – bringing you out this morning,' said Robert. 'Good afternoon. Dorothy, isn't it?'

'Good afternoon,' Dolly answered nervously.

'No distance to your house, Doctor Ford. It's when I have to deliver three or four miles.' The postmistress went across to the telegraph instrument and began to take down the message.

'Do you understand morse?' asked Robert. He was aware that the girl was trying to conceal the letter she held. He counted out some coins. 'I'll leave the change here for you, Miss Vernon. Fivepence halfpenny, that's right, isn't it?' He smiled at Dolly. 'No lessons this afternoon?'

'We have permission, Doctor Ford. We're only missing needlework.'

Robert patted her on the shoulder kindly and went out. Miss Vernon completed her message and came back to the counter.

'A penny stamp, please, Miss Vernon.'

The postmistress looked towards the window. 'I was just thinking . . . I suppose it's too late to catch the Doctor now. There you are, my dear . . . he might have been going past the old cottages. I'll have to shut up shop and take the telegramme myself.'

'We could take it for you,' offered Dolly.

'Oh no, that wouldn't be right.'

'We could go that way. Really.'

'Mrs Pennington wouldn't like it.'

'If it's important . . . it is wartime. Everyone does unusual jobs in wartime.'

'I'd leave it until after I close but Tom Webster's package is arriving from London on the four thirty-two. Mrs Pennington wouldn't like it, Miss.'

Dolly put the stamp on her letter. Miss Vernon saw that it was addressed to Captain Peter Williamson and thought, Mrs Pennington would like to know about that.

'It's an emergency, isn't it?' pressed Dolly. 'It would be foolish to leave it.'

Miss Vernon wrote out the telegramme, put it into its envelope, sealed it and handed it over to Dolly.

The four girls gathered together, arguing.

'Suppose we're seen and reported.'

'We're just as likely to be seen and reported for breaking rank *here*.' (They hurriedly assembled themselves in pairs.)

'We're helping out. Especial circumstances. You know that in especial circumstances we have to use our initiative.'

'What do you say, Madeleine, you're in charge.'

'If we go to the old cottages we have to pass the *aerodrome*,' said Dolly. 'They might be going up!'

'We might even see the one with the blue eyes,' said Phyllis.

'At least half of them have blue eyes!'

'Be a sport, Madeleine.'

'We wouldn't *speak* to anyone, even if one of them spoke to us.'

Madeleine hesitated. Her freedom was important. She was here for some time, after all. It would be unwise to jeopardise it, and yet. . . . Dolly held up the telegramme.

'I said I'd take it. I'm not breaking my word even if I go alone. It could be a matter of life and death.'

'That is right,' said Madeleine. 'If we are seen let it be the lady in the post office who is in trouble.'

'Quick . . . march!' said Betty.

It was with slight apprehension that they walked in the direction of the aerodrome. It was necessary to pass the church and the possibility of the Vicar emerging at that precise moment, or of Mrs Burder returning to the Vicarage from a parish visit made them increase their pace until they were safely by.

'That hazard's over,' said Phyllis.

'Unless we were spotted from a window.'

'The old world and the new,' said Dolly, pointing. With tremendous noise a plane took off and just for a moment it appeared to hang above the one-horse bus that travelled twice weekly between Fairwater Edge and Tolmere, the nearest town. Faces could be seen at the windows, peering upwards.

'Let's hope there is no friend of Madame's on board,' Betty said, when the sound of the engine had softened and it was feasible to speak again.

'I'd be utterly terrified to go up, wouldn't you?' asked Phyllis, watching the plane.

'Nothing would induce me. They're awfully brave.'

'My brother's dying to be old enough. He's going to volunteer for training.'

'I'd rather stick to a bicycle.'

'I'm not even allowed one of *those*,' said Dolly bitterly.

Madeleine was not listening. Her eyes were on the sky, marvelling as the machine went into a deliberate nose dive.

'Care for a spin?' asked a voice behind her.

The four girls turned as one. Cadets Will Kent and Nigel

Jessop, handsome in their uniforms, recognizable from church, stood smiling not more than a yard away.

'No thanks,' said Phyllis, blushing.

'It's terrific when you're up there,' said Will. 'You've no idea.' He looked at Madeleine.

'We have to go. Come on.' Betty began to walk away.

'Seen you in church,' said Nigel. 'Boring chap, your Vicar. Can't give a decent sermon. You girls brighten our Sundays. I'm Nigel Jessop, by the way. How d'you do?'

Betty and Phyllis giggled.

'I'm Betty Stephens,' said Betty boldly, then giggled again.

'Phyllis Hawkes.'

'Are you two nameless?'

'We have to return,' said Madeleine. 'I am in charge.'

So she *is* a member of the staff, thought Will. Aloud he said, 'How about a spot of tea? The farmhouse puts on quite a decent spread. Scones, and lashings of cream.'

'Dare we?' asked Dolly.

'Please. No,' said Madeleine. 'I will be in trouble. Already we are out of bounds.'

'Come on,' Nigel said 'We don't want to get them into hot water.'

'Hot water?' Madeleine looked puzzled.

'A colloquialism. On the spot. On the carpet.'

'Madeleine's French,' Betty explained.

'But she knows "out of bounds." '

'You soon learn "out of bounds" at Fairwater House!' They were all walking now, past the cobbler's shop, past the Elizabethan terrace of cottages (this was the oldest part of Fairwater) where the telegramme was to be delivered, on past the farm with its notice *Light Lunches Cream Teas*. Will took out his wallet, removed a piece of paper from it and fell into step beside Madeleine. Without speaking he pressed it into her hand, and with his own, bent her glove fingers over it.

'We *could* have tea,' said Phyllis wistfully.

Madeleine turned her head to speak to Will. He quickly

released her hand and took a stride that placed him between Dolly and Phyllis. 'No,' he said. 'We don't want to
get your . . . Madeleine, is it? . . . ' He looked back at her
and their eyes met. 'We mustn't get you into trouble.'

'Hot water!' said Madeleine.

Madame Marie Pennington sat in her study, her head in
her hands. Robert Ford stood before her, looking down at
her smooth, brown, neatly parted hair, drawn back in two
soft wings.

He said, 'My dear, you simply must not take it like this.'

She looked up. Her mouth was tremulous. 'It seems as
if my whole life has gone.'

'Come now, Marie,' said Robert, slightly irritated.
'That's too dramatic. Even for you.'

'No, no. It is true. You are the only person in the world
who knows anything about me. When James died . . . if it
had not been for you . . . and now you say, like an excited
boy, you expect *me* to rejoice with you.'

'You must look at it my way,' said Robert, sitting beside
her on the chaise longue and taking her hands. 'And remember, I'm not going to fight. Fight to save lives, yes. It's
my profession, it is my *vocation*.'

'Like mine is teaching,' she said bitterly.

'I never intended to stay here. If my mother had not
died when she did I would never have gone into partnership
with my father. I was trapped.'

She did not like it. She changed her approach. 'What are
we going to do now, here, in the school?'

'You'll find someone else to deal with the measles and
the colds and the bruises caused by hockey sticks!'

'But what will *I* do without you?'

'You will write down all your problems and keep them
for me to solve when I return on leave.'

'And after the war?'

'Perhaps by then I shall be content to become a big pillar
holding up a very small community.'

She began to cry, and Robert felt tempted to go on

ruthlessly, to tell her he might very well go and work in a big hospital in a working-class area in one of the industrial towns. Instead he said, 'You must learn to remain calm. Listen, I want you to overcome your fastidiousness.' He stood up and took from his pocket the cigarettes he had collected earlier from Miss Vernon. 'These are quite mild. I have had them made up especially for you. They will help you control your nervous disposition.'

He opened the flat box and held it out to her. Madame paused for a moment, and then, courageously, took one and put it between her lips. Robert watched encouragingly, opened a box of matches and struck one for her. 'Breathe in,' he instructed, '. . . now . . . that's right . . . see how it relaxes you. Don't hurry, don't pant, in slowly . . . exhale.'

At the very moment Madame finished her first cigarette and pressed the stub into a silver ashtray held out to her by her doctor, Dolly opened her purse and took out the telegramme. The four girls stood at the foot of the school drive and looked at one another in horror.

'Give it to me,' said Madeleine. 'I'll take it back. You three must go in.'

'You dare not.'

'No one will miss me. *Hurry*.'

Dolly gave her the telegramme, overwhelmed by gratitude and a certain amount of shame. She, who had engineered the whole excursion, had allowed herself to forget its *raison d'être*, and all because of the cadets. How the other sex clears everything from one's mind, she thought. Her passion for her brother's friend, the Captain Peter Williamson to whom she had been writing secretly all term, had waned as she had contemplated taking tea with the dashing young fliers. 'You hurry, too, Madeleine. If anyone asks where you are I'll say you dropped your glove.'

Madeleine watched them walk away and disappear from view at the bend of the drive. She turned and began to retrace her steps but after a few minutes she stopped and folded back the cuff of her glove. She withdrew the minutely

73

folded piece of paper and opened it carefully, recognizing it as she did so as Gertie's note, passed to her in church. *Nuns are forbidden to look at their own bodies*, she read. She puzzled over it, then recalled the conversation as they had waited at the gate. It had concerned Doctor Ford. He had listened to her heart, Millie had claimed, and Gertie had giggled and asked if it had been through her chemise. It was not difficult to follow the train of thought to this feeble note that had caused so much mirth. Perhaps it is because I am a year older, thought Madeleine, or perhaps it is because I am French, but Gertie strikes me as a very silly girl. Only Dolly came close to her and there was something about Dolly that made Madeleine just a little ill at ease.

The sound of approaching hooves at a rapid trot caused her to step aside. Doctor Ford was in the saddle, and although he must have seen Madeleine he did not call out a greeting but rode past, urging his horse still faster. Clearly he had come from the school, small doubt that he had been with her relative. It was possible that, like Madeleine, he did not particularly wish to be recognized. When he had gone from sight she looked down again at the foolish note Will had pressed on her and was on the point of throwing it into the ditch when she saw that there was writing on the other side. *I would very much like to see you alone*, she read. The words were followed by an address.

Madeleine delivered the telegramme and asked the young labourer's wife if she might borrow a pen and paper. In the simple front room she sat at the table and pressed down upon the velvet cloth, choosing her words carefully, hoping that her English spelling was correct.

'Thank you for bringing it, Miss,' said the woman. 'Though I'm not sure thanks is what I mean. He's determined to go, you see, and nothing I could say would change him.'

Madeleine thanked her in return and put on her gloves again, and carrying a different envelope left the cottage. Ada saw her from the window next door and was quick to tell Ida when they met next morning in the school kitchen.

Later Edwin Reed saw her as he bicycled back from the Vicarage where he had taken a basket of vegetables and fruit. Gertie saw her from the dining room where she had been waiting anxiously the last quarter of an hour.

'No one asked,' she whispered, as Madeleine hurried to hang her coat on its hook. 'You seemed gone so dreadfully long.'

'It did not seem long to me,' answered Madeleine, and peeled off her galoshes.

On the last morning of term Matron stood by the open linen cupboard as the girls lined up with folded blankets and bedcovers. At the top of the stairs luggage all but blocked the way down. Madeleine, whose blankets remained on her bed, had difficulty stepping round Phyllis's expensive trunk more suitable for a cruise liner than for the charabanc which waited to take it to the station. (Miss Cadogan said as much to Miss Darke as ten minutes later they watched the coachdriver do his best to stow it.)

'Are you the last?' said Matron to Gertie, checking her list.

'Yes, Matron. Everyone else is downstairs.'

'Then there is a blanket missing.'

'Perhaps you miscounted them.'

'Perhaps I did,' said Matron with a sigh, and began to count them again. She hoped to leave that evening for her sister's in Scotland and resented any delay.

This being the Christmas holidays, even those girls with parents overseas had been invited to share the festivities with relatives or friends. The staff, too, were departing. Miss Craig was joining her married brother in Oxfordshire; Miss Cadogan's widowed mother was delighted that Miss Darke would be accompanying them to midnight mass on Christmas Eve in the little Norman church where it was reputed that King Richard II had once taken sanctuary.

'I can't wait to be on our way,' Miss Darke murmured as she lined up the girls to board the charabanc. 'You'd better have help,' she called to the perspiring driver, as he hoisted Phyllis's trunk yet again into the baggage compartment behind the let-down panels along the side of the vehicle. She sent Gladys to fetch the gardener from the kitchen where Cook was giving him his mid-morning cup of tea.

The girls climbed the folding steps and scuffled for the window-seats. The driver's livery matched the maroon and cream of the paintwork. On the side, in flowing long-hand written at an angle, were the words *Fairwater Tours*. On the rear the block letters announced that private bookings were welcomed from those who telephoned Fairwater Edge 32 or called at Palmer's Lane, Fairwater Green. The gardener arrived and put his shoulder to the trunk. 'Won't go,' he said, and Phyllis heard him through the open window and burst into tears.

Miss Craig, dressed for travelling, for she was accompanying the girls to London, snapped irritably, 'There's no need to make a silly fuss. It can be fetched by cart and put aboard the next train or Messrs Carter Paterson will collect it.'

'It's all very well,' sobbed Phyllis, 'I'll have nothing to wear.'

'Don't be rude,' answered Miss Craig (a headache was beginning to bite at her left temple, just above the eye), 'and don't expect me to believe you wear your school uniform during the holidays.' The charabanc shook as the luggage panels were slammed into place and fastened. Madame came out of the house accompanied by Madeleine and the gardener went back inside to finish his tea. The driver spoke to Madame, touched his hat, jumped aboard, and collapsed the steps.

'Have a happy Christmas,' called Madame, waving as her girls were borne away. A few feet from her Phyllis's trunk resting on the gravel was a reminder of another departure that the festive season would inevitably bring.

Madeleine spent the rest of the day assisting Matron with her inventory and with replacements and repairs. 'Another hair tidy for the Pink Dormitory. There's a cracked wash jug in the Green. A stitch in this, my dear, and it will last us for at least another term.'

It was in exchange for her keep and she gave her services willingly. She had the sensation that she had done all this before, that her life in France in the small town near the Belgian border had belonged to somebody else at some other time. Her mother, her grandmother, her sharp-tempered father had so faded from her mind that her visual recollections of them came only from the photographs she had brought.

'Very neat fingers,' said Matron. 'Are all the French good needlewomen, Madeleine?'

'Not all,' answered Madeleine, smiling, thinking what a foolish question it was.

'Silly thing to ask,' said Matron as if she had heard the thought. 'It's just that you people from the Continent always seem so gifted in the domestic arts. Hats, too,' she added. 'I always remember my Aunt coming back from Paris with a *chapeau*. It is chapeau, isn't it?'

Matron left for the station at half past four and Madeleine took tea with Madame. It was already dark. They sat either side of a small folding table before the fire. It was spread with a cloth and the teapot was silver. Madame lifted a silver-domed lid from a hot dish. She spoke in French. 'These are called Sally Lunns.'

'Sally Lunns,' Madeleine repeated. 'What does it mean?'

'I take it to be a name.'

'Who was Sally Lunn?'

'I don't know. But you'll find them delicious.' Madeleine took a bite. 'It is delicious,' she agreed. 'But you know I cannot adapt to afternoon tea.'

She thought how absurd it sounded as, an hour later, while Madame rested, she took the path towards the lake. Her own cloak still hung on its peg. Millie had left hers behind and it was this that Madeleine hugged round her shoulders as she passed the Out of Bounds sign. Sally Lunn! Were all the Sallys teased as she had been. Will you have a little Madeleine? There was no moon and only the faintest glimmer from the water charted her way along the edge. From time to time she stopped and lit a match. The wind was up and almost blew out the flames. The dry bushes rustled and the bare branches hit against one another. Underfoot there were sandy ridges, funnelled from recent rain and now hardened by frost.

She reached the cave and moved aside the furze and long dead grasses. Stooping, she entered and lit a match, found the candle left in a crevice and applied the flame to the wick. It burned high and straight and Madeleine placed it carefully in the rocky niche where it cast a shadowy light. She took the folded blanket from its corner and spread it out. Then, kneeling, she loosened her hair and began to unbutton her dress.

Will's hand touched her shoulders, caressing them. He kissed her hair, took her fingers from the buttons and completed the task himself. She turned her head to face him, their eyes and then their lips met and he laid her gently down on the blanketed ground. He covered her with his greatcoat, asking, 'Was it hard, this time, to get away?'

'Easy.' She held out her arms to him. 'The girls are all gone. There was no one to lie to.'

He was cold and soon held her close under the thick coat. 'I have been given Christmas leave.'

She asked in despair, 'Do you go away, Will?'

'To my people in Oxfordshire.'

'For very long?'

'They've given me fourteen days.'

'Must you stay fourteen days?'

'They'd think me a pretty rum fellow if I didn't.' He kissed her again then and for a while they did not talk. Afterwards she said, 'When you come back . . . how long?'

'Before my solo?' He felt her nod against his shoulder. 'Not long.'

'You know, I would like so much to fly with you.'

'I would be the happiest man in the world.'

'Is it very wonderful to fly?'

'It is like being set free.'

'Like an angel,' she said. 'We would be two angels flying.'

'Not, I hope, for half a century yet.' He raised himself to look down at her loved face. 'After the war, will you marry me?'

'I would like it to be now.'

'You see, I'd be all set, being twenty-one in June. But you'd have to have permission from your people.' He kissed her forehead. 'You're awfully young, Madeleine.'

'How I am going to miss you, my darling, for fourteen terrible days.'

'I wish I could take you home for Christmas. We have an awfully jolly time, tree, carols and all that stuff. First-rate grub too!'

She smiled up at him, not understanding all that he was saying, and outside in the darkness Ada and Ida, arms linked, chores done, hurried home along the sandy path.

On Christmas Eve they were like two widows in the church. They sat among the other women of the parish and Marie Pennington thought, he is out there in France, tending the dying in the trenches. I am lost without him. Please God let him return. Said Madeleine to herself, how shall I exist during the empty days ahead. (Four days already seemed like four years.) The Reverend Burder stood before the decorated altar, before the holly and the ivy and the nativity scene his children had made and said to them in exultant tones, 'Behold! We must rejoice!'

The London train pulled in to the branch line station in the late afternoon of 16 January 1915. Miss Darke and Madeleine stood on the platform to welcome back the girls for the Lent term. Outside in the yard the charabanc waited. (The driver had ascertained that Phyllis's trunk was being sent by road.) The engine steamed to a halt and already the excited pupils were letting down the windows, leaning out and waving.

'Ah! Youth!' said Miss Darke as they began to scramble down. 'Don't jump,' she called out. 'Move *decorously*, Gertie!'

'I'm about as decorous as a sponge cake,' said Gertie.

'Don't you mean decorated!' The girls who had been fighting back their tears at Euston Station were now stifling their mirth. Miss Craig descended. 'I hope you enjoyed your vacation, Miss Darke.'

'Oh I did, Miss Craig. I trust you did also.'

'And Madeleine,' said Miss Craig as an afterthought. 'How did you find your first English Christmas?'

'It was very interesting, Miss Craig.'

'I'm afraid mine was touched by sadness. My brother suffered a slight stroke.'

'I'm so sorry, Miss Craig.'

'I must attend to the baggage.' Miss Craig walked briskly down the length of the platform to where the two elderly porters were unloading the trunks and cases which only a month before had travelled in the reverse direction.

Dolly, Gertie, Phyllis, Betty and Gladys gathered around Madeleine.

'Did you have good hols?' 'Was it lonely without us?' 'Were you on your own, you and Madame, just the two of you?' 'Did you have a goose for your Christmas lunch?'

Madeleine greeted her friends warmly.

'Come along,' cried Miss Darke. 'Less gossiping. Find partners and line up as quickly as you can.' They separated into twos and formed a shambling line, not adjusted yet to the discipline of the school crocodile, still chattering excitedly.

'You are not a flock of magpies,' said Miss Darke. 'You are young ladies. Please modify your voices accordingly.'

'Madeleine,' begged one of the younger girls, 'may I be your partner?'

'Another time. Walk with Ruth.' (The girl groaned.) 'There's a new girl over there, standing on her own. She must be feeling quite left out.'

Madeleine walked over to the solitary figure. 'You must

be Florrie Brown,' she said. 'I am Madeleine. We are in the same dormitory.'

Florrie, miserable in her immaculate uniform, looked at Madeleine through her thick-lensed spectacles. Her own eyes were magnified considerably, and they signalled desperation.

'I would like you to be my partner,' said Madeleine. 'We are about to walk to the coach.'

'Oh thank you,' said Florrie. Thus the adoration, which was to prove so trying, took root.

'Leaders, please start.' But the line had only just turned through the arch into the yard when a military ambulance with a canvas top and a red cross on the side pulled up alongside the charabanc, and two stretcher bearers jumped out and ran into the station. The guard must have been waiting for them, for he directed them up into the train, and a moment later a young VAD nurse stepped on to the platform, to be followed by the stretcher bearers carrying between them a soldier whose face was almost wholly concealed by bandages, and whose splinted arm lay outside the red blanket covering him. The nurse bent and spoke to the man who apparently answered her in a satisfactory manner, for she straightened, and smiled and rested her hand on his shoulder.

As they passed beneath the arch, Miss Darke told the girls to stand aside to make way. They pressed back against the wall as rapidly, but with care, the bearers conveyed the wounded man towards the ambulance. Eighteen pairs of eyes looked down compassionately. One girl, who had lost a brother during the holidays, began to cry. Several, thrilled by the proximity to the drama of war, clutched a neighbour's sleeve or hand.

'Poor chap,' Miss Darke murmured to Miss Craig.

For a moment the stretcher bearers paused as the VAD hurried ahead to open the door of the ambulance. Madeleine found her eyes inextricably locked to those of the man lying below her. It was a moment of extraordinary poignancy and power. Her sympathetic glance had been prolonged, trapped almost, by the gaze of the soldier and it was impossible to look away. She had the sensation that their eyebeams were tangible, that if she tore hers away it would cause physical pain, further wounds. His eyes were dark and they sent forth such signals of anguish Madeleine was both touched to the heart and stricken by fear. Then the men moved on and the eyes could no longer bore into hers. She felt as if she had been cut free. Released, she turned to speak to Florrie. The ambulance doors slammed, the engine started and Dolly's voice rang out a revelation.

'I thought I recognized him! I've just realized! It was Doctor Ford!'

At teatime there was much excited chatter. One girl had attended her sister's Coming Out dance and recounted her partners' conversations. Others had visited theatres, enjoyed Christmas parties or been bored by family gatherings. Everyone had some tale to tell and only Florrie, the new girl, saw Ida slip a note into Madeleine's hand as she handed round the rock cakes (there were always cakes on the first day of term). Madeleine did not read it but put it quickly into her cardigan sleeve and at once turned to Florrie and drew her into discussion. Had she stayed away from home before? (No) Did she think she would be – how did one call it – homesick? (No) Did she want to come to boarding school? (Yes) And as she bit into her rock cake and found it hard and crumbled it on to the plate, Florrie thought how wonderful it was that she had found a friend who was so devastatingly beautiful and interesting and interested, and who received secret messages with incredible poise. She wondered what the missive could contain and guessed at its importance. Later, unobserved, she watched Madeleine take it out from its hiding place and eagerly read the contents. Later still (when Madeleine was asleep) she crept out of bed and put on her glasses and read it herself, afterwards replacing it carefully exactly where she found it.

He was wounded! He was home! Marie Pennington had not slept the night before and at the morning assembly her mind was not on the announcements she was making about the arrangements for the new term, the hockey match that had been organized with St Hilary's in Tolmere, the shocking discovery of mouldering cakes behind the wardrobe in the Blue Dormitory during the holidays. At least he was safe and he was alive. She concluded with a heartfelt prayer for the return of loved ones from the Front and Gertie and Dolly (who had already discussed the matter) exchanged glances as they knelt side by side.

'I am going to walk into Fairwater,' Madame said to Cook, 'to complain to Henry Brown of the quality of the mutton he sent for supper yesterday. I noticed that several of the girls were compelled to leave pieces at the sides of their plates.'

'I hear the Doctor's back,' said Cook. 'Will you call?'

'I had intended to do so,' answered Madame, her heart thudding fast.

She went first to the post office to collect her cigarettes. She had not persevered with the habit but knowing that he was home and would ask her if she had obeyed his instructions the purchase had a painful pleasure.

Miss Vernon was a source of the information she desperately sought. 'You probably know it, Mrs Pennington. Wipers, isn't it, where the battle was?'

'I know where you mean.'

'Lottie told me she'd heard from the War Office to expect him back. I delivered the letter, I knew there was something . . .'

'Please go on. I am very concerned.'

'Dr Chevington's been over from Tolmere already. She says he was wounded on the second day. There you are, fivepence halfpenny. I made them mild.'

'The second day?'

'He was with a boy in the trenches, cutting off his leg or something shocking, when the whole thing blew up.'

'Have you heard if he was very badly hurt? Miss Darke tells me he was carried on a stretcher, bandaged from head to foot.'

'I saw him carried in.' Miss Vernon gestured towards

the little window with its view across the green. 'He can't be that bad, can he, or they wouldn't have allowed him home?'

'I shall go over immediately,' said Madame Pennington, passing the coins across the counter and placing the cigarette packet in her handbag.

'Oh, he won't see no one, Mrs Pennington. No one at all. Very morose, Lottie says he is. Good morning, Annie,' she said as Ida's mother came into the shop.

Madame exchanged greetings and hurried out. Both women watched her as she walked towards the doctor's house.

'He won't see her,' said Miss Vernon. 'But she won't take my word for it. Lottie was up with him all night.'

'She's sweet on him,' said Ida's mother.

'Always was,' agreed Miss Vernon. 'Even before her husband passed on,'

'Husband?' said Ida's mother with a smile.

'That's idle gossip, Annie and you know it. There never was evidence to the contrary.' She paused, her eyes on Madame Pennington, now knocking at the doctor's door.

'The Doctor didn't care for *her*, though,' pursued Ida's mother, loath to let the subject drop.

'Taking down the telegrammes you can't help knowing what's not meant for your eyes,' said Miss Vernon.

'Of course you can't!'

'There was that lady up in London. Married from what I could make out. They went abroad just before war was declared. There!' she finished triumphantly. 'I told her. She wouldn't believe me. Always thinks she knows better.'

They stood in silence as Lottie closed the door and Marie Pennington walked disconsolately down the path.

In his dream Robert Ford found himself looking again into Madeleine's eyes. When he woke the moment stayed with him and he said to himself, who is she, who is she? Then the recollection came and he said aloud, 'Marie's ward,' and he opened his own eyes to the moonlight cutting through the small mullioned window of his bedroom and lighting the wall beside his bed. He was in pain and could not move into a comfortable position. He stretched out his hand and felt for the handbell on the night table, rang it without giving a thought to the time. It was five minutes before Lottie came in answer, tying the cord of her thick wool dressing-gown.

'Help me sit up, Lottie. I can't sleep.' She turned up the gas light, raised him against his pillows.

'Shall I make up the fire?'

'I'm warm enough.' He asked her for a book and told her to go back to bed, then had the grace to apologize for calling her at such a late hour. 'Forgive me, I had no idea of the time.' As if to remind him the church clock struck eleven. When she had gone he looked at the printed page, but the words made no sense. What was her name? He let his head fall back as if he were again on the stretcher and saw the fretted roof of the station arch, the pale faces turned down towards him with no more substance than shadows. He felt himself come to rest and looked up, drawn into the grey irises and locked within the dark centres. She had penetrated his soul.

He started awake, aware that he was enduring a kind of fever, that the drugs he had taken to ease the pain conjured up the images in his brain. The remains of the fire stirred and fell into the grate, leaving only a few burning embers. Of course! It was Madeleine. She had said, 'My cousin's daughter is coming to join us. *Madeleine*. It is the least I can do.' If she had stayed in France, seen the horror, the terror, the death and the mutilation . . . *Madeleine*. He picked up the book again and forced his eyes to the page, but he read little more than a paragraph before his lids drooped and he heard a voice from a long distance calling out her name.

Will took her in his arms, held her so close against him he could feel the beat of her heart.

'I can hear your heart,' said Madeleine, and he wondered if perhaps it was his after all.

She ran her finger round the stubble on his chin. He was fine haired and it was only a year since he had found it necessary to shave every day. It gave him a feeling of pride that she could feel the growth, and he put his hand over hers and traced the line across his upper lip, then pressed his mouth into her palm.

'I thought I would never see you again,' she said. 'Every day I walked along the path and once I came inside here and sat on the blanket and cried.'

He said, 'I love you so much. My mother couldn't understand why I wanted to get back.'

They kissed, then she whispered, 'Will you run away with me?'

'If it wasn't for the war. I can't run away from that. One has to finish that.'

'When it is finished it will be too late. I will be made to go back home.'

'Not if I have anything to do with it,' he assured her robustly. 'I shan't let you go.'

She said, 'I have not heard from my parents, Will.'

'Don't worry, my darling. I expect the letters just aren't getting through the lines.'

'You do not understand me,' said Madeleine. 'For me now I would rather they were dead.' She drew him down to her and for a moment his ardour was stilled by the impact of her words. Then she added fiercely, 'Without you *I* should die,' and he was overwhelmed by the intensity of her love.

Florrie stood at the dormitory window and waited. Dolly stirred in her sleep from time to time and Gertie snored, but neither of them had woken as she kept her vigil. At last she saw the figure of Madeleine on the lake path, walking swiftly, appearing and disappearing as she kept close to the shadow of the trees. She wore her cloak and Florrie shivered as if it were an apparition fading in and out of the night shadows. The cloak and the moonlight gave that illusion. Quickly Florrie pulled the thin curtain across, placed her glasses carefully on her chest of drawers and climbed into bed. She lay on her back and listened for the soft latch of the garden door and the creaks on the stairs. Madeleine, ascending, paused on each tread, poised for discovery, her explanation already contrived. A door opened and a shaft of light illuminated the step above her. She flattened herself against the wall, heard the murmured voice of Miss Darke and caught a glimpse of Miss Cadogan attired in a white nightdress as she closed her bedroom door. Miss Darke passed along the landing and Madeleine, shoes in hand, fled up the last few stairs and into the dormitory. A night-light burned in a saucer of water on the washstand, and in its glow Florrie, her lids half down, watched her unfasten her cloak, revealing her nightdress underneath. Without her glasses Florrie could not see the features clearly but Madeleine's eyes were brilliant in the pale surround of her face. She bent to turn back her sheet and as she did so those bright eyes caught Florrie's and forgetting to feign sleep any longer Florrie held the shocked and horrified gaze, thrilled at the sharp intake of Madeleine's breath.

'You can trust me,' she whispered fervently. 'I will never betray you. I swear I will never tell a soul.'

Madeleine held her French Conversation classes in the art room. On this particular afternoon rain fell upon the sky-lights and the electric light had been switched on although it was not yet three. Millie, Gertie, Phyllis, Dolly and Betty sat in a semi-circle by the dais on which there was a single upright chair. The easels had been moved to one side, charcoal sketches still on them. It was easy to see that the sitter for the portraits had been Madeleine, although the talents of the artists were varied. She had sat upon the chair, her hair loose and falling well below her shoulders. Now she stood before them, her hair ordered into what was known, appropriately, as a French pleat. She found it easier to converse, she told them, if she walked about the room.

'Has any one of you,' she asked in her own language, 'visited France?'

Dolly answered her in halting French, 'I visited Paris when I was a little girl.'

Madeleine paced the length of the shelves which were jammed with jars of powdered paints and brushes, shells, fossils and dried flowers. She looked at Dolly as if she expected her to go on.

'When I was six years old,' Dolly added after a long pause.

'Tell me about it,' said Madeleine.

'Why don't you tell *us* about it?' Betty asked, and smiled.

Madeleine said, 'I have never been to Paris.'

'I was wondering,' Betty went on, still smiling, 'if your accent is good enough to teach us. I mean, we don't want to acquire a country burr.' She said it in English.

Almost as she uttered the last word the door opened and Madame stood on the threshold.

'Madeleine, I wish to talk to you immediately.

'While I am gone,' said Madeleine with a glance at Betty, 'Dolly will tell you of her experiences in Paris.' And she followed Madame out.

'In my study. It is very serious.' As soon as they were in the room Madame began to speak very fast. She was trembling. 'I am very distressed. You must tell me the truth. I must know exactly.'

'Of course.'

'Today it was reported to me that there has been a liaison between a cadet from the flying school and one of my girls. That they met last term when you were permitted to go on a shopping expedition. Is it true?'

Madeleine nodded.

'If it should become common knowledge you realize that the school would have to close.'

'The meeting was of no significance,' said Madeleine. 'The cadets approached us, spoke to us. That was all.'

'I'm afraid not,' said Madame. She looked straight into Madeleine's eyes. 'They were seen meeting for tea. Unchaperoned. Once at the farm and twice in Tolmere. Did you know that?'

Madeleine put her hand on the back of a chair to steady herself. 'No.'

Madame sat down. She was close to tears. 'I know I can trust you. Advise me. Shall I punish Dorothy alone?'

'Dorothy?' asked Madeleine in a whisper.

'Were the others involved? No parents would send their daughters to me if . . . if. . . .'

'Do you know his name?'

'The cadet's name? Of course I know his name. I have written to his Colonel.'

'There were two who spoke to us, I just wondered . . . '

'Kent. William Kent. I cannot allow you to go out again with the prefects, you realize that? You have not answered me. Was it Dorothy only?'

'It was only Dolly,' said Madeleine.

'Shall I send her away? Believe me, I do not want her in the school.'

'I think,' said Madeleine, 'it would do more harm if you made her a public example.'

'I shall remove her prefect's shield. She shall have no senior privileges. You look upset, Madeleine, but please understand, I am not blaming you. Go back to your class, my dear, and send Dorothy to me.'

That night Dolly wept. She lay with her face in the pillow, muffling her sobs. 'It isn't fair,' she gasped. 'We only had tea. I could die. I feel so humiliated. She's going to take my badge away in front of the whole school.'

Gertie came and sat on her bed and stroked her hair. 'Do you love him, Dolly?'

'Of course I do. He's wonderful. The most wonderful person I've ever met. She's only taking it out on me because she can't get her precious doctor to propose.'

'Don't be unhappy,' Gertie begged. 'I think you were brave and courageous to defy convention. To meet him in secret.'

'And now I'll never be allowed to meet him again,' Dolly managed to say, shaken afresh by crying. 'I shall never see him except in church . . .'

Madeleine sat up in bed and said, 'Dolly, try not to make so much noise. Matron will hear you.'

Florrie looked from one to another of them but said nothing.

The morning of Will Kent's solo flight was fine, a clear, cold, bright day with the frost turning each blade of grass into a silver bodkin. With his instructor he taxied round the field, the surprising heat of the winter sun penetrating his thick leather flying jacket and warming his cheeks beneath the goggles. He turned out of the glare and brought the plane to a stop. His instructor climbed out of the rear cockpit, thumped Will on the back and shouted 'Good luck!' as he jumped down. Will just caught the words over the noise of the engine, raised his gauntleted hand in response and turned the plane into the wind to take off.

Gaining height he saw Fairwater like a relief map below him, the barracks, the church, the oval of the village green. The sunlight that had warmed him on the ground dissipated in the icy wind which crept round the velvet edging of his goggles and made his eyes water. He circled over the aerodrome and thought how neat it all looked, the other aircraft lined up on the bumpy field, the hangars, the tarpaulin tents. His instructor stood looking up, his face a pink dot encircled by the leather helmet, a tin toy. The farm, too, was out of a nursery, model barns, gates, sheep and cows. A train stood in the station, and Will saw a group of figures on the platform before he checked his oil pressure gauge and turned so that his flight would take him directly over the school.

He had been flying low and Miss Vernon, taking down a message from her telegraph machine, found the sound was blotted out by the engine of the plane. Doctor Ford, his bandages removed that morning by Doctor Chevington, crossed to the window to look out, envying the man up there his solitude and freedom. In the station the police officer from Fairwater Edge helped the guard and the porter unload his new Douglas motor-cycle combination from the van. It looked splendid, even under the partial wrappings, a tribute to the machine age and to the diligent saving from his wages. He felt a surge of irritation as the words of admiration uttered by the porter, Tom Clegg, were drowned by the din of the overhead plane. (Motor-cycle engines were one thing, aeroplanes another. 'God,' he told his wife later that evening, 'never intended man to rise above the earth.') In the Blue Dormitory, Matron had to raise her voice for Gladys to hear her. 'Never,' she cried, 'never never never let me find you using another girl's comb again!' On the hockey pitch Miss Cadogan was umpiring a game.

There they are, thought Will. The teams of girls reminded him of one of those games you worked for a penny on the pier. You turned a knob and the players hit the ball. Unless you were skilled it usually disappeared behind the goal. He tried to identify Madeleine who had complained to him that she was compelled to play, but he was too high to distinguish one girl from another. He could not single out the glorious auburn of her hair – or Dolly's fair plait. He flew on over the school house, turned across the lake and came back deliberately losing height, determined that not only would he see Madeleine but that she would also recognize him.

The low sun cast long shadows from the trees, giving the impression of a summer evening. Now he could pick out detail, the skylights in the roof, the bushes that concealed the entrance of the cave, the gate through which he passed on those night excursions to be with his beloved. He followed the line of the drive, his eyes on the field beyond. He could see the ball, the red and blue team bands diagonally across the white shirts. He could see Madeleine! She looked up and in that moment he had a sense of exultation close to ecstasy. He thrust the nose of his plane upward so that he could soar into the cloudless canopy of the sky. He had a second's revelry in the sheer joy of flight and then everything went out of control, his world spun and his life ended without a glimpse of the expected spectacle of war.

The noise was devastating. First came the terrifying roar of the engine so loud that Matron threw Gladys to the floor and then flung herself protectively on top of her. A mile away Miss Vernon left the telegraph instrument tapping out morse and ran to the post office door. On the hockey pitch the girls ran screaming and sobbing to the corners of the field. Only Madeleine stood frozen, her gaze still directed up as the plane tore through the tops of the elms, the fuselage disintegrating leaving the tail empennage jammed in the high branches as the cockpit crashed to the ground. Out of it hung the twisted body of Cadet William Kent.

'Inside girls. Inside at once,' shouted Miss Cadogan. She put her whistle to her lips but could not gather the breath to blow. Like a sheepdog she ran, ushering the girls ahead of her into the house. Madame was crying into the telephone in the hall. 'Robert, please come. It is terrible, terrible.' She broke into French. 'Oh my God, he must have been killed. I plead with you to come.'

Florrie broke away and rushed upstairs. On the landing Matron was holding a glass of water to Gladys's lips. Florrie dashed into the dormitory and snatched her camera from a drawer and collided with Gertie and Millie whose panic had given way to thrilled curiosity. They both ran to the window to watch.

By the back door Dolly was crouched, huddled and shaking. 'Cook,' Miss Craig was demanding as Florrie rushed by, 'prepare plenty of hot sweet tea!'

Florrie was prevented from approaching the drive by Police Constable Best, who by chance had been visiting Ida. Already he had marked off the area by lengths of string, and was awaiting the arrival of his superior. In the meantime he was suitably officious. The half hour following brought first Mr Burder transporting the Doctor in his trap. He trotted up the drive at a spanking pace, Robert Ford hunched in a heavy army greatcoat in the rear seat, his bag on his knee and a stick in his hand. Next came the military ambulance and Will's Instructor, ashen faced, and the Colonel, driven in an open car. Will's body had been released from the harness and lifted into the ambulance as the police officer dismounted from his bicycle, inwardly cursing that his new motor-cycle had not been ready to ride. 'An hour later and she'd 've been on the road,' he said angrily to Billy Best. 'It may sound harsh but this unfortunate accident happened sixty minutes too soon.'

With the exception of Edwin Reed the villagers came on foot. 'He just seemed to emerge from the bushes,' said Florrie afterwards. 'He just seemed to be *there*.' She had managed to find a way to creep close to the severed cockpit and point her camera at it from three different angles. 'One at least ought to come out.'

Madame, deeply distressed, had emerged from the house as the ambulance drove slowly away. She saw Florrie at once and sent her briskly indoors. The police officer went over to her. 'Very distressing, Ma'am. I hope your young ladies are not too upset.'

'His poor parents,' said Madame, her eyes filling. The police officer answered with sympathy, 'The penalty of war.'

'He was not involved in war.' Robert Ford spoke harshly. He leaned on his stick and Marie Pennington could not look at the uncovered scars on his face.

Ida and Ada hurried out with trays of tea, smirking with self-importance as they offered the refreshment to the Vicar and the Doctor and the Warrant Officer and the members of the RFC and police force. 'Not *you*,' said Ida sharply as Edwin Reed stretched out his hand towards a cup.

Doctor Ford drank his beverage and replaced the cup on Ada's waiting tray. Then, without a word, he nodded and began to walk with some difficulty down the drive. Madame hurried after him. She caught his arm. 'Please, Robert. The girls need attention.'

'I am no longer in practice,' he said, not slackening his pace. 'You must call someone else.'

'But I cannot reach Doctor Chevington at this hour. He will be on his rounds.'

'The girls will survive.'

They reached the curve of the drive where the villagers still stood surveying the wreckage, turning the tragedy into a kind of social occasion.

'Mrs Pennington,' called out the butcher's wife, 'this is a dreadful thing to have happened in the school grounds.'

'They are private grounds,' said Robert Ford, 'and you are all trespassing.' He said to Marie Pennington with his old compassion, 'Go back indoors. Your nerves will not stand much more of this circus.'

She was on the point of answering him, begging him again to return with her, when she saw Madeleine kneeling by the tree. Her arms were wrapped around herself and she was shivering violently, her lips trembling, her teeth chattering.

'Madeleine, what are you doing here?' To the Doctor she gasped, 'I was told they were all in the house,' as if he would reprove her for lack of care.

'Go indoors,' said Doctor Ford. 'You will catch cold.'

Madeleine turned her head towards him, her eyes met his but she was not aware of the contact. Then she put both her hands to her face, covering it. She shook as if she were crying but she made no sound. Robert Ford had a great desire to turn away from her but instead he took her hands from her eyes and led her towards the house.

There were two beds in the white-painted sick room. Over the gas fire hung a picture of the Madonna and child, respectably and respectively robed and swaddled. Dolly, who had taken a sedative, lay sleeping, her breathing heavy. Madeleine's eyes were closed but she was awake, listening to the popping of the fire as the wind blew in the chimney and to the murmur of voices, Matron's and Doctor Ford's, on the landing outside. An aeroplane passed overhead and the sound was agonizingly painful, both to her heart and her throbbing head. Perhaps Matron sensed it, because she opened the door and looked in. 'Both sleeping peacefully, Doctor,' she said, and their footsteps walked away.

Madeleine knew she had not slept and yet she did not know how long she had been lying there with Dolly still unconscious in the other bed. She had been aware that Matron had come in and drawn the curtains and for some minutes had stood looking down at her. She had heard her turn down the gas fire. Opening her eyes now Madeleine saw that it gave out a faint blue glow, and in that dim light she watched the door open and Florrie slip inside, come across to her on silent bare feet and take her hand. She had not the strength even to return the pressure of Florrie's fingers or to utter the smallest acknowledgement of her presence.

Florrie whispered, 'I had to see if you were all right.'

Slowly Madeleine turned her head to look at her. The flame from the gas fire danced on her glasses. Madeleine's eyes filled with tears.

'Oh, don't cry,' said Florrie. 'Don't cry, Madeleine.' There was a note of triumph in her voice. 'I knew it was him.' She stroked Madeleine's dry hot forehead. 'You must not think about it. Don't cry.'

Matron was framed in the doorway, her starched cap outlined like the rising crest of an angry bird. 'How dare you come in here. Go back to your dormitory at once. I will report you to Madame in the morning.'

Florrie stalked out, her head high. Matron went over to Madeleine and wiped her tears away.

'You must not allow yourself to be upset. It was a terrible accident but we did not know the poor boy. It's not as if he were a dear brother . . . Mary Forsyth lost her brother . . . or even. . . .' and she glanced across at Dolly's bed, shaking her head at the memory of that dishonourable foolishness.

Florrie had the qualities of leadership but preferred to remain solitary. Gladys, drawn by the sharp featured face, the large eyes magnified by metal framed glasses, had attached herself, sitting beside Florrie at mealtimes, begging to be her partner when they went for walks. This afternoon, to Florrie's irritation, she had asked permission to go with her to the darkroom to watch the latest photographs being developed.

'I wish you'd leave me alone,' she said angrily. 'You know I like to do things by myself.'

'But I want to learn how to do it,' Gladys said. 'And Madame likes us to do things in twos.'

They stood together in the darkroom in the glow from the red lamp and watched the images appear, dark and indistinct. 'Drat,' said Florrie. 'Look at that.'

Gladys leaned forward. 'Perhaps there's something wrong with your camera.'

'It's a jolly good camera, you idiot. It cost ten bob. It was the rotten light that messed up the pictures, not the camera.' She peered critically at her results. 'This one's not too bad though.' Just discernible, at the base of the elm tree, was the shattered cockpit.

'I think it's horrible,' said Gladys with an admiring shudder.

'But he's not *in it*,' snapped Florrie. 'How can it be *horrible*? They'd taken him *out* by then.'

The undertakers came from Tolmere to collect the body and transport it to the station. Four horses with black plumes nodding above the hedgerows drew the hearse, and men in the fields and women in their gardens saw the plumes and stood in upright respect until the sound of the wheels informed them that the sad burden had been carried past. In the station yard the small procession halted. The Colonel who had walked alongside removed his hat, and the four bearers, in top hats and long black coats, lifted down the coffin. The train was approaching and smoke rose above the station roof.

Will's remains were borne beneath the arch onto the platform where the porter removed his cap, torn between social convention and the anxiety to get on with his work which at that moment was to help unload the mail.

The train creaked and steamed and clanked as the simple coffin was carried aboard and the mail bags thudded onto the platform. It took no more than five minutes. The guard blew his whistle and waved his green flag and jumped up into his van. The undertaker's men relaxed and shook hands with the Colonel and as soon as he had walked briskly off, they took off their hats and strolled out towards the empty hearse. Before the cortège had moved away the brisk trot of Miss Vernon's pony was heard on the cobbles, and she turned smartly into the yard, calling out to the porter that she had arrived.

There were two small sacks for Fairwater and Miss Vernon, used to manual work (her boy had gone off to France), heaved them into the cart, refusing help from the porter. 'I'm younger and stronger than you are, Tom Clegg!' She said much the same every day. It was only as she was about to climb up into the driving seat that she saw Madeleine, pressed back in the waiting-room doorway, gloved hands clasped, her head low. The postmistress recognized her at once as Mrs Pennington's ward and wondered what she was doing alone at this time of day. She left her pony tethered and walked over to where Madeleine stood. 'Like a nun,' she said later to Lottie. 'In that long cloak, her head bowed.' Miss Vernon's sister had taken orders and it was a posture with which she was familiar and heartily disliked. She believed in holding up your head in this world and looking folks straight in the eyes.

'Like a ride to the village, would you, Miss?'

Madeleine raised her head but did not speak.

'It's cold for walking,' said Miss Vernon cheerfully.

'You'd best get up in my cart. Just mind the bags as you go.'

Still without a word Madeleine stepped up into the cart and sat shivering, her hands again gripping one another as if the action gave her actual support. The postmistress put a rug over her knees, took her own seat, said, 'Hold tight!' and urged her pony into an energetic trot. There were people waiting for their letters, some of them no doubt important, and Clara Vernon did not believe in wasting anybody's time.

Madeleine did not look up as they passed the aerodrome, although she heard the sound of an engine and in her imagination saw the aeroplane and the young men surrounding it. She thought of Will and the physical and spiritual void drained her of energy. She could not have stood or spoken or lifted a hand. Her eyelids closed of their own volition and the side of the little cart supported her. It was thus that Robert Ford saw her from his bedroom window as Miss Vernon turned her pony into the cobbled stable yard beside the post office. He saw her extend her hand to help Madeleine descend, saw her put her arm round the girl's shoulders and lead her indoors, saw her come out alone to unharness her pony and unload the postbags and hoist them up as a man might to take them in.

Madeleine sat on the upright chair which Miss Vernon had brought from her parlour behind the shop. She had no strength to remove her cloak or her gloves. Indeed, it had not occurred to her that she should, she did not even recollect that she had them on, could not have told you at what time she had risen that morning or how she made her way to the station. For herself she had ceased to exist. When Miss Vernon reappeared from behind the counter with tea in her best cup and saucer, Madeleine, prompted by instinctive habit, put out her hand to receive it but her fingers failed to grasp and the china fell from her hand and shattered on the floor. The hot tea against her leg, the sound of the teaspoon clattering on the stone flags sent hot tears springing to her eyes. She fell on her knees and ineffectually tried to scoop up the broken fragments.

'Don't you worry about that. I'll see to that,' said Miss Vernon and she lifted Madeleine to her feet and drew her into the back room.

The post office was empty when Doctor Ford entered. The bell attached to the door rang and it took him a few seconds to adjust his eyes to the dim light.

'It's dark today,' he said as Miss Vernon came from her parlour. 'You need to light your lamps.'

'Oh Doctor Ford, there's been no time to do anything. I'm that glad you've come over.'

He dissembled. 'Oh? What is the trouble?' His gaze was directed at the open door.

'One of the young ladies from the school is here. She's poorly. Would you come through, Doctor. Oh, I'm grateful to see you, I really am.' She lifted the hinged flap of the counter and gestured that he should come through.

He had never had occasion before to go into her parlour. It was a curious room, half workroom, half home. There was a cabinet with drawers, each labelled with the names of tobacco, and on the top there were a number of cigarettes recently rolled. Two packets had already been made up and sealed and he saw the name 'Pennington' written neatly on the lids. There was a noisy grandfather clock, its pendulum visible behind a glass fronted door. There was a bureau with a glass fronted bookcase above, and in the seconds in which his eyes took in his surroundings he saw Doctor Johnson's Dictionary, a copy of Shakespeare, Mrs Beeton in red morocco leather and a set of Dickens, all of which he was sure had been the property of Miss Vernon's late parents. There was a round table covered by a plush velour cloth with a fringe, ledgers piled high on it, a paperweight and sealing wax and scales beside them. There was also a small, firmly stuffed settee and Madeleine was lying on it. Her cloak and gloves had been placed on a bentwood chair, her hat rested on the seat and her boots had been placed neatly on the floor alongside. Doctor Ford now saw nothing but the girl. Her hands lay inert and her eyes were closed.

'Here's Doctor Ford to see you,' said Miss Vernon. 'Isn't it fortunate he came in to the shop. I haven't even asked him what he came to buy.' To Robert she added in a lower voice, 'She all but passed out, I had to hold her up, just bringing her in here.'

He went across to Madeleine and looked down at her, and as he did so her eyes opened as if they had been pulled up by twin strings, a doll's mechanism. Their eyes met but she registered nothing. He took her wrist and counted her pulse beats and her eyelids flickered and closed again. He laid her arm down gently, and turned his back to her. He said to Miss Vernon, 'Unfasten her blouse.'

Miss Vernon opened the buttons on the high-collared school blouse. Underneath Madeleine wore a chemise, fastened by small pearl buttons. She hesitated, uncertain whether to continue the task. The shop bell rang and through the open parlour door Robert saw Edwin Reed enter.

'What shall I do?' asked the postmistress, referring to the chemise.

'Go, woman, go,' said the Doctor impatiently, thinking she was concerned about the shop.

She hurried out and he knelt down beside the unconscious girl, placing his ear over her heart. Two buttons pressed against the scar on his cheek. He was aware of the texture of the cotton material, the warmth of the flesh underneath. He heard nothing but her heartbeats and felt himself engulfed by immediate sensations. He acted like a man in a dream and yet there was a deliberate determination in his behaviour that he found himself questioning again and again as he lay awake during the following nights.

He looked round. He saw Miss Vernon at the counter, taking out a sheet of stamps, heard the murmur of her voice as she read the note that Edwin had handed to her, saw Edwin's dark and darting eyes attempting to look within.

He blocked Madeleine from their view. Rapidly he unfastened the buttons on the chemise and pulled it open wide, gazing down at her, overwhelmed by her beauty. He did not know how long he knelt there, he did not hear the shop door close, only Miss Vernon's footsteps behind him.

Hurriedly he rose to his feet and walked to the window which overlooked the small vegetable garden. He stared out, seeing nothing. He said, 'Inform Mrs Pennington that she must arrange a conveyance. The patient must on no account walk. Tell her that Doctor Chevington will take over the case.'

Miss Vernon hastily buttoned the chemise. Madeleine's eyes opened but he walked by without glancing at either of them.

For a week Madeleine lay in the sick room, suspended between reality and dreams. Each day Marie Pennington came to sit with her and one afternoon she took Madeleine's hand and said, 'I have some news for you that will make you feel better.'

'As long as it is not another medicine,' said Madeleine, and for the first time she smiled.

'You will be able to write to your mother!'

'I have written it must be twenty times,' Madeleine answered, her weariness returning. 'There is no way to reach her.'

Matron came in, very brisk and starched. She attended to her own caps and aprons and had once held Madeleine to her bosom but it was like being pressed to a sheet of paper.

Madame said in English, 'I have been telling Madeleine the good news. My late husband's cousin is an acquaintance of Lord Northcliffe, and he has arranged for Madeleine's letter to go in the official dispatch to France.'

'Well, let's hope it has given her an appetite,' said Matron. 'She's been eating enough for a baby sparrow. Do you have restaurants in France, Madeleine?'

'Yes, Matron.' She looked at Madame and suppressed a smile.

'Then give me your order. Cook's made a lovely hot-pot. Or there's Mr Brown's sausages he brought up fresh this morning!'

He could not prevent himself, he lacked the power to keep away. It was as if he were drawn by some force as strong as gravity. In one of those hours when he thought he had overcome it he compared his nocturnal visits to Newton's apple unable to resist the pull of the earth. There were whole days when he was able to contemplate his meals with pleasure, to think about riding again when his arm was strong enough, to enjoy a short winter walk. But when the image of Madeleine obsessed him his mind was empty except for thoughts of her. Then he would set out with his stick and take a surreptitious route into the grounds of the school and in the shelter of the trees would wait and watch and sometimes he would see her. He watched the windows and the doors. He had seen her cross behind the drawn curtains of her dormitory; he had seen her pass the stair window on her way down to supper; he had seen her sitting at table and, in her silk tunic, take part in the Greek Movement class. For that he had come out of his covert and pressed close against the wall. It was like looking into an optical toy, a lighted box, where a goddess danced among shadows. His mother had had a little theatre from her own childhood with which she had allowed him to play. There had been among the characters a top-hatted doctor with a black bag (he had called it Father) and Persephone with flowers in her hair. A mechanism of slides, mirrors and revolving drum allowed him to set the doctor on his course or Persephone gathering spring blossoms. A candle (always lit by his mother) bathed them in a golden light and he often wished he could alter the sequence of their action, turn the brisk doctor away from the front door or Persephone from the mouth of the underworld. He had wanted to introduce the two figures, have the doctor attend to Persephone's cut knee (he had been no more than six or seven at the time) and it seemed to him now that he too was controlled by the turn of the praxinoscope, for ever isolated from the world. Standing in the gloom of the February dusk he thought he was a projected figure knocking silently on a symbolic door. Madeleine was always out of reach.

102

He had been seen but not recognized. He was thought to be a ghost. Phyllis had reported the first sighting: 'A sort of shadowy outline at the edge of the drive. It just disappeared into the trees. My heart almost *stopped*.'

They assumed it was Will. 'He was cut off in his prime,' said Gertie, 'like Hamlet's father. Doomed for a certain time to walk the earth, you know.'

They knew. They shivered as they looked out of the windows and believed they saw the apparition. The news spread through the school, the teaching staff heard the rumours and shook their heads at the credulity of their pupils. Miss Darke alone had misgivings. 'There are more things in heaven and earth,' she murmured to Miss Cadogan as they trudged together along the lake path on their free afternoon. 'This,' said Miss Cadogan, 'is firmly rooted in the schoolgirl imagination.'

Ida and Ada, schoolgirls no longer, were less dismissive. One Monday washday, bed linen boiling in the huge copper, the air of the wash-house thick with condensation, they fed soaked sheets through the mangle and discussed what they had heard.

'I durstn't walk down there at night an' that's a fact,' said Ida.

'Ghosts don't 'appen that quick, Miss Dolly says. Takes years.'

'She don't know nothing,' snapped Ida. 'Miss Phyllis seen him. Miss Madeleine too. That's what turned her head.'

The washerwoman, pattens on her shoes, wrapped around with a sacking apron, her big arms as red and damp as her face, soon put an end to their gossip. 'I'll turn you into ghosts if you don't pin them sheets up quick.'

They staggered out into the small flooded yard, a basket of sheets and pillowslips between them. The water flowed along a gutter and into an open drain. Steam rose up from it and thinned in the air like the lake mist on a summer morning. Ada and Ida lowered the heavy basket between two long washing lines and began to hang up the sheets. 'White as ghosts,' giggled Ida nervously.

'There's one, but 'e 'nt white,' said Ada, and Ida dropped her end of the sheet onto the sodden ground. 'I was on'y joking,' Ada promised. ' 'Tis Doctor Ford.'

They both turned to stare. He was some distance away, keeping close to the trees. He wore his army greatcoat with the collar turned up against the chill morning, and he leaned upon his stick at each step.

'Maybe someone's took ill then,' Ida said after a pause.

' 'E don't 'ave 'is black bag, silly.'

'He's sweet on Mrs Pennington. Do you think they be having a secret meeting then?' They almost dropped another sheet with laughing.

The figure moved into the shadow and stood looking at the house. 'Stop loafin' about,' shouted the washerwoman who had to complete her work and be at the Infirmary at two. The maids put their heads down and heaved up the last sheets.

'My mam do say,' whispered Ada, 'since 'e come back 'e's been as cheerful as a wet wash day.' Stifling their giggles they ran back into the wash house, the empty basket bumping between them.

Cook believed in the importance of afternoon tea. Each afternoon when Mrs Pennington had received hers in the study, nicely laid on the silver tray, and the young ladies were seated in the dining room, she presided over the kitchen staff. 'Fetch the kettle, Ida. I'm sure Mr Wilkins won't say no to another cup.'

'No I won't, Mrs Parsons,' said the temporary gardener who was too old for fighting (and for gardening too, Cook thought), 'and I could fancy another slice of cake.'

'They say there's going to be rationing of food,' said Ida, bringing the kettle from the black leaded range.

'We'll 'ave to make the most of Mrs Parsons's cakes, then, won't we,' said the gardener. 'While we still got 'em.'

'There won't be no shortage of food *here*,' Cook answered disparagingly. 'Maybe in *London*, but not here.'

'Do you believe in ghosts, Mrs Parsons?' asked Ada.

'No I don't, miss, and neither should you. Ghosts is heathen.'

'We saw one this morning!'

'Oh, I know what those young ladies have been saying. You'd think they'd been better raised. That poor young gentleman going to his maker and they have nothing better to do than. . . .'

'Oh it weren't 'is ghost, Mrs Parsons, 'twas Doctor Ford's.'

'Doctor Ford's not passed on though, 'as 'e?' asked the gardener, startled.

Ida sat down again, and giggled. 'We saw him standing down by the trees. It's his spirit. Dreaming on Mrs Pennington.'

'You're a wicked girl, Ida Briggs. You can take your plate into the scullery. You're lucky you've bitten into that seed cake or I'd keep you on bread and butter. I won't have talk like that at my table.'

Ida picked up her plate and went out, pleased to have riled Cook. She shut the door behind her and looked out of the window. She had no doubt at all that she saw Doctor Ford, flesh or spirit, dissolve from view into the darkness of the trees.

Robert walked towards his home. His leg ached and the healed wound on his face was taut and burning. The Swan had opened by the time he reached Fairwater Green (if he had been asked the route he had taken he could not have said), and voices reached him through the open door. A good fire burned inside and for a moment he thought he would go in and drink a glass of brandy to give him the strength for the last stretch. But since his return from France he had not been sociable and the prospect of a cheerful landlord, of deferential enquiries as to his well being, of subjecting his scar to close scrutiny from men who had been his patients, was too great an ordeal. His steps were slow as he went up the path to his front door.

Lottie heard his key turn and came from the kitchen to

greet him. 'Oh Doctor, I was wondering where on earth you'd got to. Are you all right? I'm glad to see you home safe and sound.' She intended her tone to be light but anxiety was apparent in her eyes.

He said, 'I walked further than I intended.'

'You must have done. Look at the clock. I didn't know whether to keep your dinner in or out of the oven.'

'You may set the table, Lottie.'

He made the attempt at being in control, but his fingers fumbled at the greatcoat buttons and he staggered a little and put out his hand to the mantelpiece.

Her voice was compassionate. 'Let me help you off with your coat.' She pulled it gently from his shoulders and helped him to a chair. 'I'm going to fetch your dinner in here and set it on the little table. You look all in.'

She opened up a gate-legged table, fetched a cloth, talking continuously. 'There was two callers this afternoon. Mrs Mendip to ask for jumble. I said the Doctor's in no fit state to start rummaging for your jumble stall. But she kept on so in the end I gave her the cruet your sister sent and which you said was so ugly you didn't want to see it no more. I hope I did right.' He managed to nod. 'I hope your sister don't expect to see it. But she never do come here for anything more than a cup of tea.'

The last sentence or two she called out from the kitchen. Then she was back with a slice of meat pie and boiled potatoes and winter cabbage. She set it down, edged the table an inch or so closer to him, and handed him a napkin.

'Then Mrs Pennington called. She said she'd been to the dressmakers and just wondered how you are. You are going to drink your glass of stout, ain't you, Doctor? Doctor Chevington said on no account was you to miss your glass of stout.' She moved the glass in reach of his right hand. 'She said she thought you'd like to know the young lady is feeling stronger.'

The sensation of fear seemed to fill his chest and throat. He was aware that his hands were shaking, that his mouth tasted bitter. When the words came they were rasping, he had no means of stopping them. 'You may tell Mrs Pennington that I am not concerned. You may tell her to cease calling. You may tell her that if the *young lady* goes into a decline, falls into the lake or turns consumptive it is of no possible interest to me. I cannot eat. My appetite has been driven away. Oh God, Lottie, help me.' He recollected himself, gripped the arms of the chair. 'Help me off with my boots.'

Flustered and concerned, Lottie moved aside the table and knelt down to help him.

The night was the worst he had known, worse even than when he lay uncertain whether he would live or die, whether they would amputate his arm, whether he would ever return to his home. Now, lying in the bed that had seemed his ultimate haven, he could not sleep. Again and again he tore open her chemise and pressed his lips to the flesh he had exposed. He entered a realm where nightmares racked him although he did not dream. His wounds smelt and ran with viscid pus, repelling her so that she struggled to be free of him, sick with terror and disgust. His blood smeared her and she wept. Her eyes bore into his, pleading with him. Her eyes! Her eyes! He was borne beneath her on the stretcher and her eyes lanced him with pity. Pity me! I am hurt. My will has gone.

At dawn, he dressed. Lottie had cleaned his boots and they stood at the front of the stairs. They appeared like feet severed on the battlefield. When he put his own feet into them he felt them to be still detached. They marched him out of the house into the cold dark beginnings of the day, past the aerodrome where the planes stood like predatory birds, devourers of young men. They took him by the farm fields and he saw the cowherd taking in the cows to milk and the shepherd among the new lambs. When he reached the school drive, Robert crossed a ditch and made his way secretly into the grounds.

He took up his usual position, shielded by the trees, the thick undergrowth hiding him. He watched the milk cart clatter up the drive, saw Ida and Ada approach from the lake path and help the milk girl carry in the churns. It was five thirty. He replaced his watch and waited for the gardener to take in the coals. Light streaked the sky and other lights appeared in windows. Smoke rose from the chimneys. Dormitory curtains rattled back from the windows. Her room. Her curtains. Miss Vernon's cart came next, making an early morning delivery, the mail in a leather pouch. He stood, immobile. Through the long stair window he observed the girls descending for breakfast, saw *her*. Saw Madeleine.

She stopped. She waited. He began to shake, the sweat was cold on his face and palms. She came close to the glass. She had seen him. He said her name aloud, his eyes fixed on her face as she looked out at him, then very slowly began to unbutton her shirt. He cried out to her not to go on but the sound of his voice was lost in the rushing of the wind.

He lay on the ground. A light rain was falling but it was some time before he regained full consciousness, knew where and who he was. He put out his hands and felt the rough, damp ground, saw the branches and sky overhead. In the distance he heard a school bell ringing, girls' voices. He struggled to his feet, brushed down the particles of grass and leaves which stuck to his clothes, froze as Ida came from the back door and emptied an enamel basin of slops down the drain. She glanced in his direction and hurried back inside.

He forced himself to look at the stair window. The small leaded panes obscured the view of anyone within.

Billy's father, Charlie Best, owned the only cab in Fairwater Green. Robert hired it to take him into Tolmere, had the horse pull up before a terrace of fine houses which dated from three-quarters of a century before.

He had attempted to smarten himself, had changed his suit and shaved, but there was a cut on his chin and a drawn and haggard look about his eyes which did not deceive Doctor Chevington as he was shown into his consulting room.

'My dear fellow!' said Chevington, immaculate in his frock coat, his gold pince-nez on a cord and placed in his top pocket, his perfectly arranged cravat marking him down as a Victorian. He came from behind his desk and offered a chair. 'Sit down. Sit down.'

Robert took the seat and Doctor Chevington returned to behind his desk, sat, rested his fingertips together.

'Trouble eh? Well, only to be expected. Your system took a nasty beating. Arm playing up?'

'No,' said Robert.

'Bowels playing up? You look groggy, Ford.'

Robert spoke with effort. 'I have not come to see you about myself.'

'By the look of you it would be better if you had. Not to put a fine point on it, you seem done in. Done in. I shall prescribe whatever you say. Doctors are the worst patients. I say it myself.'

'I am here to ask your opinion,' said Robert slowly and carefully. 'One of Mrs Pennington's pupils seemed to me . . . seemed to me . . . I'm sorry.' He put his head in his hands.

Doctor Chevington went quickly to a cabinet, took out a flask of brandy and poured a measure.

'Come along now, old chap. Put this down.' He watched as Robert drank it, gasped, and seemed to gain composure. 'I am going to read you a homily, sir. Proper sleep. Proper meals. Eat all that your good woman puts before you. I have treated men with your symptoms. War shock. The inner wounds.'

Robert shook his head. He grasped the Doctor's hand. He spoke with urgency. '*I must have your opinion of her.*'

Doctor Chevington stared at him. 'My dear fellow. Of *whom?*'

'Miss Maurel. I recommended her to your care. I see now that I should have attended to her myself. I realize she has a most delicate disposition. I did wrong to reject her.'

Doctor Chevington put his hand on Robert's shoulder. 'You did right. You are your own patient for the time being and must have your sole care.'

Robert rose to his feet. 'How is she? I must know if she is fully recovered.'

'Let me set your mind at rest,' said Doctor Chevington. 'There is nothing the matter with her. The French are an emotional race and God endowed her with a full portion.' He was startled by the fevered look of his patient, the flushed skin, the bright eyes that seemed about to spring from their sockets. When Robert cried out, '*Did you listen to her heart?*' he spoke calmly as if he was pacifying a disordered mind.

'Sound as the clock up there,' said Doctor Chevington cheerfully. 'Now I'll give you an opinion of a different nature. Girls should not be educated away from home. Mrs Pennington has introduced the game of hockey. It will interfere with child-bearing. Mark my words!'

There were grilled kidneys for breakfast at Fairwater House Academy. They bled into small squares of toast. As Ida lifted the metal dome from the dish and placed a kidney on Miss Darke's plate, the mistress surveyed it with a look close to terror.

'I simply cannot bring myself to consume an organ with such a function,' she whispered to Miss Cadogan. 'I follow Mr George Bernard Shaw.'

Miss Cadogan was hungry. She cut a portion. 'One cannot be squeamish in wartime.' With a smile she leaned forward and with a deft movement flipped Miss Darke's breakfast on to her own plate and was rewarded by a grateful smile.

Millie saw and drew Phyllis's attention to it. 'Too poetic to eat base meat.'

They were permitted only to speak French at Madeleine's table. 'Français,' whispered Florrie so that Madeleine could hear. Later she asked with perfect syntax, 'Do you have a partner for church?'

Ida, having served the staff, brought a fresh dish of kidneys to the table.

'Bon vieux kidnees!' said Gertie, convulsing her friends with giggles.

'Quesque c'est "kidnee" vraiment?' asked Gladys.

They all looked at Madeleine for an answer but she had turned very pale. She pushed back her chair. 'Excusez moi . . .' Running was not allowed in the Fairwater House Academy but she all but ran from the dining room.

'She looked *dreadful!*' said Gertie. 'Someone should see if she's all right.'

'I'll go.' Florrie asked permission from Madame and followed Madeleine up the stairs to the bathroom, where she was kneeling by the lavatory being violently sick.

Florrie stood just inside the door, watching helplessly. Supporting herself against the wall, Madeleine pulled the chain then sat down on the bathroom chair, white and shaken.

'I imagine it was the kidneys,' said Florrie.

Madeleine nodded.

'Are you coming down again?'

'I can't. Please tell Madame I am unwell. I must be excused from church.'

She returned to her dormitory. The beds were unmade and the washbowls had not yet been emptied. The sight of the soapy scum made her stomach heave. The chamber pot, too, was full.

Madame came in and led her to the bed, helping her to lie back on the pillows, taking off her shoes. 'My poor girl. I will ask Doctor Chevington to call.'

'There is no point,' said Madeleine. 'He tells me it is an hysterical malaise.'

'Then I will persuade Doctor Ford. In the meantime you must sleep.' She stroked her ward's head.

'I am sorry to cause you so much trouble,' said Madeleine, so quietly Madame had to lean forward to hear.

'My dearest girl!' Marie Pennington felt close to tears. 'I have wondered how we all managed before you came.'

She kissed Madeleine's damp forehead. 'I must prepare for church.' And she covered her ward's shoulders with the blankets and hurried out.

Madeleine opened her eyes with a start. The empty beds were made and she saw Ida emptying the basins and the pot into the enamel bucket she carried on her round. She had a single cloth and Madeleine watched her wipe first the chamber pot and then the four tooth glasses and place them over the newly filled water carafes. Madeleine moved and Ida jumped, guiltily.

'Oh, Miss. I'm sorry if I woke you. I tried to be ever so quiet.'

'I was not deeply asleep.'

'Feeling better, are you, Miss?'

'Yes. A little.'

Ida came close to her. 'My Mam could help you, Miss.'

Madeleine smiled. 'I have medicine from Doctor Chevington.'

'She helped Missus Pardoe, Miss. 'Scuse me saying so, but everyone round Fairwater comes to my Mam.'

'Not to Doctor Ford?'

Ida shook her head. 'My Mam makes her special teas, Miss. Will you go and see her?'

Their eyes met. Ida blushed, looked away and shifted from one foot to the other. Then Madeleine nodded. 'I'll tell you when, Ida.'

Ida picked up her full pail and went out.

Robert Ford was among the first worshippers in the church that Sunday. Kneeling, he heard the arrival of the school and hastily sat back in his pew to watch the girls pass along the aisle. Most of them he had attended at some time or other and knew by name, Dolly, Millie, Betty, Gertie.

Where was Madeleine?

One by one they took their places. Gladys, Phyllis, a girl with glasses he did not recognize; Miss Darke, Miss Cadogan, Matron, Marie Pennington herself. The cadets followed, their boots ringing on the flagged floor. Unable to contain himself a moment longer, the Doctor leapt to his feet, sending his hymnal spinning to the ground. He rushed from his pew and confronted Madame as she knelt, her head bowed on her gloved hands, pulling them from her face.

Startled she rose. 'What is it? What is the matter?'

'They are not all here.'

'What do you mean?'

He tried to be composed. He pressed his hands to his side, kept the fingers from clenching. He thrust himself close. 'The girls are not all here this morning.' His voice was cracked.

She answered in a whisper, 'They are all here except for my ward who is not well.'

He became aware that he was the focus of attention, that the girls were watching, that Miss Vernon had leaned across to Lottie and that Lottie was nervously plucking at her hat. He turned abruptly and walked back to his pew, looking to neither side. By the time the Vicar's procession appeared the disturbance had passed.

At the end of the service he accosted her. 'I must speak to you, Marie.'

She said to the girls, 'Please go ahead and wait outside.' She looked at his ashen face, his desperate eyes and her heart was heavy with pity as she remembered him before he had gone to France. He had cared about his clothes but now they seemed scarcely to fit him.

He said, 'It is about your ward. I have spoken to Doctor Chevington.'

'Please,' she said, 'do not concern yourself. Do not be so upset.'

'He assured me she is perfectly well.'

'Doctor Chevington is unsympathetic. Very unsympathetic.' She spoke firmly. 'She does not want to see him again. I had hoped you might make an exception and visit her.' At the same time she thought that the care of another might help him recover himself.

'No.'

'If I ask you as a favour, as a friend?'

'I will not see her.'

'I am worried about her. I have no one else to turn to.'

'She is not my patient. I cannot infringe medical ethics.'

'Very well,' said Madame Pennington. 'I will not ask you again.' And she went ahead of him through the porch to where her girls waited for her in line.

The cadets had gone but their Colonel bowed his head to her. 'Good morning, Madame.'

'We are to lose our flying school after Easter,' said the Reverend Burder. His flock would dwindle, but he spoke with a sense of relief.

'You may have observed we are already grounded,' said the Colonel. 'The tragic accident hastened a decision that was already being considered.'

'How you will be missed, Colonel,' said Mrs Burder. 'Quite apart from the financial help to our local people . . .'

'I shall miss my billet. Garrison accommodation will not be the same.'

'Forgive me,' said Madame, 'but I must accompany my girls back to Fairwater House. Mrs Burder. Colonel.' She smiled at the Vicar. 'Your sermon was inspiring.'

'I hope,' he said, 'that I instilled a sense of shame into the guilty hearts among us. I shall be calling next week, Mrs Pennington, about the confirmation class.'

She went down the path and the Colonel followed her and climbed in to his waiting car. Leaving his wife to discuss a Mothers Meeting, the Reverend Burder went back into the church and was surprised to find Doctor Ford kneeling alone in a forward pew usually reserved for the school.

'Take comfort. God will guide you,' he murmured and wondered why this man who had once been perfunctory in his duties should now feel the need for prayer.

Madame Pennington allowed herself small indulgences but

liked to keep them secret. She did not count cigarette smoking among them. That had been forced upon her by Robert Ford and she could not, of course, permit her girls to witness such unladylike behaviour, even when it was considered a medical necessity. Chocolate cake was a different matter, a speciality of Cook's, but far too expensive to provide for school consumption. When there was a knock at the door that Sunday afternoon, she finished her mouthful and carefully placed her napkin to conceal the cake on her plate before she called out 'Entrez!' and picked up her teacup as if she were merely enjoying the beverage and nothing else.

Gertie and Dolly entered, Dolly still penitent a little way behind.

'I hope it is important,' Madame said, 'because I do not like to be disturbed on Sundays at this hour. It is my day of rest too.'

'Oh it is,' said Gertie. 'What the Vicar said this morning, Madame, well those of us not going home at Easter. . . .'

'Slowly please. And start again.'

'Mr Burder made us feel we were not doing anything to help our country, Madame. Those of us not going home for the holidays wondered if we could raise money for the war effort.'

'In what way, Gertie? I hope you have nothing vulgar in mind. We cannot have a sale of work or anything of that nature.'

'We thought of having an Easter Egg Hunt,' explained Dolly quietly. 'With an entrance fee for the Red Cross. Or some other really worthwhile cause. Oh Madame, please say yes.'

She hopes to regain her prefect's badge, thought Mrs Pennington and she said, 'Preparations must not interfere with your school work.'

'We thought we'd all contribute a tenth of our pocket money, to buy the eggs. You know, like the Biblical tithe. And decorate them.' Gertie added, 'It was Dolly's idea.'

Madame looked at her and smiled. The girl had suffered

115

more than her behaviour had warranted. For a second she recalled the night she had run away with Major Pennington and had been punished with no more than homesickness.

'It is a splendid idea, Dorothy. I give my consent.' The girls bobbed and thanked her. When the door had closed behind them the headmistress poured a second cup of tea and uncovered her chocolate cake.

Very early on the morning of Saturday 3 April, the eggs were delivered from the farm along with the milk. Ida was raking out the stove and Ada was carrying out the ashes when the farm cart pulled up by the door and Ada, as she always did, rolled the churn across the gravel and then hurried in for jugs to take the milk.

'I'll take the eggs,' said Ida. 'All white, I hope, like was ordered.'

'Take a look,' said the dairymaid who had packed them herself, and one by one she lifted down the wooden boxes in which the eggs were packed in straw.

Ida wiped her hands on her sacking apron and, piling the boxes on top of each other, she carried them indoors and up the stairs to the art room where the brushes and paints had been set out. Light was filtering through the skylights, and Ida had a great desire to pick up a brush or a stick of charcoal and take one of those smooth white eggs and draw a face on it. Never mind, she consoled herself, I'll wait till I get home tonight and I'll do one for Tommy for the morning. (Tommy was her youngest brother, aged three.)

She made her way down the attic stairs to the dormitory landing, and she stood listening to the morning sounds, birds outside, the cistern creaking and Gertie's snores. It was to that particular door she crept, and she waited for a quieter outward breath before she raised her hand and tapped very gently, so gently that only someone already awake and listening would hear it. Almost at once it opened and Madeleine in her nightdress slipped out, holding the door shut behind her.

'Do you have it?'

Ida put her hand in her apron pocket and took out a dark glass bottle about three inches high. In a moment Madeleine had taken it from her, and without another word, only a nod of thanks, had disappeared inside. Ida, feeling important, ran down to finish lighting the fire.

Madeleine leaned against the door for an instant and looked at the sleeping girls, Gertie on her back, her mouth half open, her upper lip vibrating with each snore; Dolly, her long hair spread out on the pillow; pinched Florrie as still as a mouse. She was safe! On bare feet she went to the washstand and took her tooth glass from the carafe, set it down on the marble top and without a pause uncorked the bottle and poured the contents. The liquid was thin and greyish brown. Madeleine picked up the glass and drained it. She shuddered at the bitter taste, concealed the bottle beneath her mattress and climbed back into bed.

All this Florrie watched through half closed lids.

Miss Darke had agreed to help with the decorating of the eggs. But first they had to be blown. Gertie, Millie, Phyllis, Florrie and Madeleine sat round the table and carefully with pins they pierced the eggs at either end and with all the breath they could muster sent the scrambled contents into a bowl.

'Breakfast!' shuddered Gertie. 'I've been instructed to take it downstairs to Cook.'

'How disgusting,' said Florrie. She glanced slyly at Madeleine. 'Doesn't it make you feel sick?'

'It does me!' Phyllis averted her eyes from the yellow pool streaked with cords of albumen. 'It's those specky bits. Those dots of blood.'

'And you know what they are?'

'Well, I think I do.'

'I'll tell you.'

At last they had finished. 'We deserve some cocoa.' (In the holidays there were often treats such as this.)

'I do not want cocoa,' said Madeleine. 'I will stay here and prepare the paints.'

'I can't think why you don't like cocoa,' Gertie said as she picked up the bowl. 'It's very nourishing.'

'It's because she's French. The French only drink coffee.'

'And wine.'

'And Vichy water. My grandparents went to Vichy for the Cure.'

'I don't like cocoa much either,' said Florrie. 'I'll stay and help Madeleine with the paint.'

They went out chattering, admonishing Gertie not to drop the bowl, and their voices drifted up and became indistinguishable as they descended. Florrie began at once to clear the broken shells and the spilt yolks, but Madeleine remained where she was, her hand resting on her stomach. Above her, on the wall, was a reproduction of Rembrandt's *The Night Watch*.

'Is the pain bad?' asked Florrie.

Madeleine looked at her, afraid.

'I knew it was poison. I saw you drink it. Like *Juliet*. You must have loved him very much.'

Madeleine said, 'I do not understand, Florrie.'

'There's nothing to be ashamed of in wanting to die for love. I think it's wonderful.' She took off her glasses, rubbed them on her sleeve and replaced them, conjuring everything into focus, the dried flowers, the shells, the dusty skull, the pictures on the wall. Her eyes slid from *The Night Watch* to Millais' *Ophelia*. She had seen *Hamlet* with her father during the Christmas holidays. 'The lake!' she said. 'Not Juliet. Oh, Madeleine, to be reunited in death!' And she darted forward and kissed Madeleine fervently on the cheek.

'Leave the room at once!' Miss Darke was in the doorway, her dark eyes piercing, high colour in patches on her pale skin.

Florrie did not speak, but she kept her head high as she walked out and they heard her unhurried footsteps on the stairs.

'Madeleine,' said Miss Darke with a note of sadness,

'Madame does not encourage Victorian behaviour, she does not like her girls to kiss or put their arms around one another. She likes them to behave in the modern way.'

'I do not encourage it either,' said Madeleine, and she stood and began to pack the blown shells neatly in the straw.

'I understand your need for friendship. You are among foreigners.' There was no mistaking the sympathy in her tone.

'Madame is of the same nationality,' Madeleine pointed out.

'But among your peers . . . Madeleine, you cannot judge the English as I can. Florrie is not the type you should seek. This is wartime and Mrs Pennington has had to widen her doors. Her father is a Member of Parliament but he is of semitic origin. You should not make a close friend of her.'

Madeleine said, 'She is not a close friend, Miss Darke.'

'Then I am glad. Choose another companion. We will not discuss it any more.' Miss Darke picked up a jar of yellow powdered paint. 'Ochre,' she said. 'Suitable for Easter, is it not? Daffodils, new chicks, or merely as a base coat. I think the eggs are going to be extraordinarily pretty. Although the talent of our artists leaves something to be desired!'

'My Mam says you ain't to worry, Miss. You ain't to worry at all.'

'Are you certain?'

'Go on back in quick, Miss. There's someone coming upstairs.'

They decorated the eggs not only with paint but under Miss Darke's guidance with beads, grasses and dried flowers. Betty made patterns, Phyllis took as her symbol the Cross, Gertie found her expertise lay in still life. When Madeleine came back into the art room she returned to her place directly below the skylight (and *Ophelia*) and with her water-colours and a thin camel-hair brush completed a delicate scene of lake, trees and sky. (Was that tiny mark an aeroplane, Miss Darke wondered, or an imperfection on the surface of the egg?)

The click of Florrie's camera took her by surprise.

'There might be just enough light,' said Florrie, 'though I must admit so far I haven't had a success indoors.'

'Or outdoors,' suggested Millie from across the room.

Madeleine turned angrily. 'Please leave me alone.'

'I had to take your picture,' Florrie said quietly. She spoke so that only Madeleine could hear. 'I shall keep it for ever. I want to remember you always.'

The pains were worse, a sensation as if gravity were pulling at her stomach or like the undertow of the tide, dragging away the firm sand and leaving sinking holes beneath. The others slept. Madeleine lay, her knees bent, her arms wrapped round her body, her fingers pressing hard against her skin.

She was afraid. At last she could bear it no longer and left her bed as silently as she had those nights she had set out to meet Will. Not a stair creaked as she made her way downstairs and took her cloak from the peg by the garden door. She could feel the gravel through the thin soles of her slippers, but she did not dare leave the path and the protection of the house. Only when she had turned the corner and could be no longer overlooked did she take to the grass and follow the line of the spinney to the lakeside. Only when she was level with the caves did she pause to rest, and the ache in the pit of her stomach was no worse than the one already in her heart.

She gathered strength and walked on through the gate towards the village, until the church tower was visible through the trees. From time to time she stopped and crossed her arms over her stomach and waited until the pain subsided, and then she hurried on to make up for the minutes she had lost. She kept close to the church wall, past the graves and out into the lane. Ahead of her the expanse of Fairwater Green looked like water in the moonlight and as hazardous to cross.

No one saw her. She traversed that wide and exposed place and thought of the pioneers who crossed the plains of America not knowing whether Indians lay in wait. Only the red lamp burning by the Doctor's door gave her the courage to go on. She said to him later that it was her guiding star.

She pressed the night bell, waited less than half a minute and pressed it again. Then, through the convolutions of the speaking tube came the voice of Doctor Ford. 'Who is there?'

'Doctor Ford. Please come down. I am ill. It is Madeleine Maurel.'

How many hours passed before he opened the door, blocking her way in, staring at her as if she were phantom? He had dressed hurriedly, his nightshirt tucked into his trousers, his feet thrust into his shoes without socks.

'I am ill,' she said again. 'Please let me come inside.'

At last he stood back from the threshold, allowed her to enter and closed the door.

Madeleine supported herself on a chair as Robert Ford lit his surgery lamp. He spoke to her angrily. 'You have no right to be here.' He was very afraid.

Madeleine whispered. 'I cannot stand.'

He put his arm round her and lowered her on to the chair.

'Help me,' she said. 'I am carrying a child.'

'Whose child?'

'It does not matter.'

'*Whose child?*' he persisted.

She answered wearily, 'He is dead. It does not matter.' She was stricken by pain and nausea and began to vomit. He shook her.

'What have you taken? I need to know.' She stared at him. 'A village woman? Did you get the brew from her?'

Madeleine nodded and relief surged through him. He longed to comfort her but his voice was savage, his words harsh.

'Then you'll suffer nothing worse than sickness and

diarrhoea. A common complaint among the ladies of this Parish. Gin and licorice powder will not dislodge a human foetus. Twenty-four hours and the pains will have gone.'

Madeleine raised her head. 'I do not want the pains to go, Doctor Ford. *I will not have the baby.*'

'You have no alternative. The fruits of sin are not so easily discarded.'

'It was not a sin,' she said. 'I loved him. Help me.'

He took a deep breath. 'No.'

'You have the knowledge,' she pleaded.

'Do you believe in God? In the sanctity of human life?' (Did he?)

'God does not believe in the sanctity of human life,' Madeleine answered clearly. 'You saw men killed in my country. What were God's reasons for that? You were wounded. You could have saved lives. What was God's reason for that?' She began to speak in French but she was not aware of it. 'My dearest boy was killed. Why did God do that?'

She began to cry, long painful sobs and it was all he could do not to take her hands and press them to his heart.

'You must tell Mrs Pennington,' he said gently. 'She will find some place for you to stay until the birth.'

'You do not understand, I will not give birth. If you do not help me I will kill myself.'

'I cannot take life,' Robert said. 'It is against the law, my profession, my moral judgement.'

'Then the life you will be taking is mine.'

He did grasp her hands then. 'If I intervened in the harmony of nature, the danger to you . . .' his voice was shaking. 'I have seen women die in such circumstances. Pitiable deaths. Double deaths.'

She was exhausted. 'I will take my chance.'

'Give your child life. I will arrange adoption through the church. I swear your name would never be revealed.'

'If I had this baby I could never let it go. I would love it too much. You must see it has to be done now.'

He said, 'I cannot.'

She took her hands from his. 'One day I will go back to France. I will be able to send you money.'

'You believe I may be bought?'

'Forgive me,' said Madeleine weeping. 'Do not hate me. I do not know what to do.'

The first morning light pierced the window and his lamp became ineffectual. He put down his head. After a long while he said, 'I will do what I can.'

Madeleine stretched out her hand to touch his. He could not recall that she stood or that he turned to her again, only that he held her in his arms and that his own eyes were full of tears. His anguish was terrible, for her and for what he was about to do. She said at last, 'I must go back. Shall I come here tomorrow night?'

'No,' he said. 'It must be daylight.' He wanted her to say, 'It is impossible. It cannot be done.'

She steadied herself and moved away from him, fastening her cloak.

'We are to hide our Easter eggs before breakfast later this morning. I will return to you then.'

Part Three

The Answer

William MacMillan Esq, Editor
An Argosy of Mystery Tales
Magazine House
Fleet Street
London   5 December 1939

Dear Mr MacMillan

We last corresponded in 1926 so I will understand if you have
no record or recollection of it. I sent you what I will now call
Part 2 of a real life mystery which began during my schooldays.
(You published Part 1 in your Christmas issue of 1917.)

By one of life's extraordinary coincidences the conclusion to the
story was recently revealed to me. I am enclosing it herewith,
together with the earlier sections in the hope that you might
publish them, perhaps in serial form. Enclosed also a stamped
addressed envelope for your reply.

Your sincerely
(signed) Ann Oxford (Mrs)

PS Since I last wrote to you I have contributed to a number of
periodicals including those in your own group.

Mrs Ann Oxford
Hill Cottage
East Mere
Rutland   15 December 1939

Dear Mrs Oxford

I am of course familiar with your work and certainly remember
the second part of your manuscript arriving in this office in 1926.
I was a young sub-editor at the time, but was appointed editor
two years ago on the retirement of Mr MacMillan. It might
interest you to know that he had been with AMT since the turn
of the century.

Alas, I am unable to publish your complete story. For the first
time since its inauguration in 1878 we are suspending the magazine. Lack of staff (I myself am about to take up war work) and
the likely paper shortage have convinced the Management that
they have no alternative course.

Might I suggest that you offer your manuscript to a book
publisher at a later date under a single title such as *An Easter Egg
Hunt?* I do not feel the present climate would render the book
acceptable to the general public, who are looking for literature of
a more optimistic and cheerful nature. This does not imply that
I personally was not fascinated and horrified by the conclusion to
your story.

With best wishes for Christmas and to us all for the new year,

Yours sincerely
(signed) Edward Holomby-Crisp

PS It also occurs to me that in spite of the disguises you have
employed, certain of your key characters might recognize themselves. You say, for instance, that 'Madame' is now living in
Bournemouth. She probably belongs to a library!

The notice on the gate of Fairwater House read 'Evacuee Reception Centre'. It was a strange sensation to return to the school again after so many years. I had kept away from the place since my 'detective work' in the twenties although I was not living many miles away. The frustration of being unable to follow the trail further – I had met with one dead end after another – and the demands of my work and family were sufficient excuse. Besides, although I had promised Madame that I would visit her, I grew increasingly aware that my schooldays had not been the happiest of my life and I wanted to cut myself off from them. It had been painful in my search for Madeleine to 'recherche le temps perdu'!

I had lost touch with most of my old friends. Betty, I knew, was teaching in Edinburgh. Gertie had married well and for a few years sent me expensive Christmas cards. I frequently heard Florrie on the wireless, recounting her travels abroad. The BBC sent her everywhere from the Berlin Olympic Games to Hollywood, but I made no attempt to look her up even when on one occasion we were both under the august roof of Broadcasting House.

Sometimes I saw Academy girls on Tolmere station waiting to change to the branch line. The uniform had been modernized, shortened, coats instead of cloaks, shirts and striped ties in place of the high-necked blouses we once wore. There were day-girls too, by that time. Sharing a carriage with a pair of them on a summer afternoon I engaged them in conversation, and at the end of it everything seemed so utterly altered that I felt illogically that my own years there counted for nothing. Only Madame (she had become Mrs Robert Ford just after the last war and was widowed just before this) remained as a link. Everyone else had gone.

She sold the house to the local authority during the Crisis months of 1938 and retired to Bournemouth. She probably could not face another social upheaval, she had struggled so desperately to keep out the non-professional class.

Together with the other voluntary workers I was directed

into the old dining room, to await the arrival of the evacuees from Liverpool who were due to arrive within the hour. The furniture had gone and I was disconcerted by the familiar and the unfamiliar so closely allied. The curtains, the shutters, the pattern on the floor were exactly as I remembered, but there was a long trestle table bearing buns and a tea-urn where the staff had sat and a stack of folding chairs piled beneath the hatch. On the walls were a batch of the current posters put out by the Ministry of Defence, blackout reminders, admonitions to carry your gas mask, that careless talk cost lives.

One of the helpers came in with a tray of glasses and jugs (*our* jugs, those at least had remained) of bright orange squash. She put the tray down and looked at me, looked away and then back again. She was a big woman in her early forties and her hair was going grey but I was certain that I recognized her face.

'Ida . . . or is it Ada?'

'Ida,' she answered. 'Ida Best now. I don't remember your name, but I know you was here a long time ago.'

I couldn't account for the lump in my throat. I told her who I was. I managed to exchange a few facts with her, how many children we each had, where we were living now, then turned away as though I were concerned with the conversation being carried on at the other side of the urn.

'I hope they've taken the numbers into account this time. They sent two hundred to Fairbourne.'

'Ridiculous. Well, there's only accommodation for forty here, they'll have to take the others back.'

'Not even toilet trained, half of them. And never seen a cow or a sheep.'

'Poor mites!' (That was Ida.)

'Talking of mites, I've made up the carbolic. The ones at Fairbourne had hair that was *alive!*'

'Cup of tea, dear?'

'No thank you,' I said. 'I used to be at school here. I'm going to have a look round upstairs.'

130

First I went into Madame's study. It had been turned into a sort of committee room with a central table and chairs and a gas fire had been installed in the grate. I had a sharp recollection of standing there, my heart knocking against my ribs, knowing that I had done wrong, awaiting retribution from that harsh French tongue. Thank God it was all over. I looked out of the window towards the lake and saw that a safety fence had been erected, they were not going to risk drowning the evacuees! I closed the door quietly when I went out and thought, old habits die hard!

The Green Dormitory had gone. I experienced a sense of shock when I opened the door and saw three new baths in separate stalls and reeled from the smell of disinfectant emanating from a bucket. The de-lousing centre! Resting on the basin were two steel combs. Gladys, Phyllis, Millie and Betty, where are you now?

My dormitory was still there, still pink – pink curtains, pink spreads, flowered pink paper on the walls. I sat down on the bed where I used to sleep, horribly nostalgic for a time when I cried at night and longed for the comforts of home. I opened a dressing-table drawer, but it was empty. Had I expected to see my hair-ribbons neatly rolled? Had I expected, when I unlatched the door of Florrie's dark-room, to see the awed faces in the red glow, the Bible in Florrie's hand, my ribbon suspending a swinging key in order to unlock the secrets of the grave?

The room had been made into an office. The sink had been removed and replaced by a desk with an anglepoise lamp. Bookshelves covered the small walls and as I looked at the titles nearest to where I stood (Gray's *Anatomy*, twelve volumes of Havelock Ellis, *Diseases in Women*) I realized that Doctor Ford had taken it over, possibly the only place available in the house for him to call his own.

There are times when we are drawn to unpremeditated action as though compelled by outer force. Perhaps my thoughts of that distant seance had stirred a restless spirit. I was surprised myself when I slid open a drawer in the desk, surveyed the neatly sharpened pencils, rubbers, paper clips, closed it and turned the key of the cupboard underneath. There were index cards in wooden boxes (patients' notes); appointment books from 1910 until 1915, and a neat stack of diaries, the earliest written in a round schoolboy's hand. Yes, I looked at them! I, who had such scrupulous regard for personal privacy, would not read another's letter even when pressed. I learned that young Robert played truant on 8 May 1903 and spent the day in Tolmere at the fair, that he was in love with one Florrie Davies when he was not quite seventeen and that in his twenties he had some trouble rejecting the advances of a certain Mrs Pennington whose husband he was attending for a dickey heart and encroaching gout. But these were not really the entries I wished to see. The last volume was dated 1915 and I turned – or that spiritual hand turned for me – to the entry dated Easter Sunday, 4 April.

I had opened the book from the back and as the pages flicked over I realized that there was only one entry and that it had begun on that particular day. The days of the succeeding weeks, the months that followed had been overlooked, or rather, not accounted for. He had written over Holy Days and Quarter Days, days of national celebration and the autumnal equinox. It was as if from then on life had ceased for Doctor Robert Ford.

5 a.m. I simply cannot sleep. We parted only half an hour ago. I saddled the mare and sat Madeleine before me, making her lie low with her arms around Sally's neck. I covered her with her cloak until we were away from the village. I have seemed a weird enough fellow of late for an early riser to think nothing more than I was taking a nocturnal ride. She could not have walked the whole distance. I took her by my secret route to where I have kept my vigil, and watched once more as she slipped up the latch she had left undone some hours before. Home again and already I am like Faustus, half sold to the Devil. There is no Devil. My divided soul then. Warring to save either her or her unborn child. What must I do? Why am I so possessed by her? The preceeding pages are testimony to such madness of behaviour, such a swerve of direction, such loss of purpose that neither the Archbishop of Canterbury nor Professor Freud could account for it. *What am I to do?* I know already. I prayed that she would come to me. But God, not like this, not like this.

6 a.m. Lottie can prepare my breakfast and then I will send her away.

7.30 a.m. Perhaps it was a dream. Heaven knows I've suffered from delusion enough these past months. Breakfast in the dustbin and Lottie, astonished and gratified, gone to visit her brother.

2.13 p.m. She was here some twenty-five minutes after I had last written. No fantasy of the brain. I heard her knock on the front door, opened it immediately – for I must have been standing behind it – and drew her in and fastened the bolt. No one saw her. Or so she said. I went to help her off with her cloak and she held out her hand. 'I have nothing else to thank you with.' She opened her fingers and held out a painted egg, a gentle little landscape following the curve all round. I took it, thanked *her* and told her I would never part with it. Then I put it down very carefully on the desk in my surgery – whence I had guided her – and asked her to take a chair. She gazed on me with a sudden fear and mistrust, and informed me she had not changed her intention and I was to make no attempt to alter her mind.

I swear I had not planned to say it. If any plea had entered my mind it was to beg her, once again, to tell everything to Marie and to allow me to arrange adoption for the child. Instead I heard my voice saying, 'Be my wife.' She did not answer for a long while. When eventually she spoke it was with astonishment and – it is painful to put it down as it was to hear – with horror. She said, 'You cannot mean what you ask.' I went on my knees before her like a Victorian wooer. I told her I would do all in my power to make her happy. I pulled her hands which covered her face and assured her she would not regret it. She said she understood that I was a doctor and under oath to save life, that she understood my generosity, but that *I did not understand her*. I asked her if there was any other way in which I could help her which would not necessitate taking an innocent life and she answered with greath strength. 'No. There is no other way.'

I say my soul had been 'cleft in twain' as Shakespeare had it. So too my mind. I had nurtured such extraordinary passion for this girl, dreamed of her in every way, worshipping her, desiring her, degrading her with acts and images, loathing myself for secret thoughts which defiled her purity – a purity I now know to have been yet another figment of my brain. Yet in the intimacy of this other act I was about to perform she ceased to be *Madeleine* for me. I turned away while she covered herself with a sheet, respecting the modesty I had so disregarded that morning in Miss Vernon's parlour. I administered the ether to her, seeing only the frightened eyes above the pad. When she lay unconscious on the table I revealed the limbs I had imagined and penetrated her not in love or lust but with dispassionate thoroughness, emptying out her uterus as if I did not murder, doing all that had to be undertaken with a butcher's expertise. It was only afterwards, as I carried her, still inert, up the stairs to my room, that I knew what I had done and that it was my darling I held in my arms.

She became conscious only moments before the church bells began ringing. I had not left the room and was standing by the window when I heard her speak in French, very faint. She asked for a drink of water. I believe the relief and tenderness in my eyes could not have been hidden from her. She then asked me if she had spoken in her native language and I told her that she had and that she should not drink yet since it was liable to make her vomit. She wondered (as is customary following an operation) if it 'were all over'. I assured her that it was, upon which she struggled to climb from the bed, saying she must go to church. Not to atone for her sins – I myself felt need of cleansing – but to reassure Marie. She had planned, she said, to say that she had walked to clear her head and that she had not wanted breakfast. I sat beside her and told her that she must remain calm, that I would go to church and that when I came back I would concoct her story. I explained that she would have to stay in bed, even after she had returned to school. I suggested I might say I stumbled upon her during my afternoon walk! She responded eagerly to the notion. 'That I swooned! I have swooned often enough!'

From the open window we heard the sounds of marching feet. The bells stopped pealing and the commands to the cadet squad reached us clearly. 'Flight. Flight halt! Stand at ease. Stand easy!' I watched her for I had guessed the identity of her lover. She did not control her emotion. I pressed her hand and told her I must go or else half the village would call to see if I were alive. I helped her to lie down again and said she should sleep while I was gone. She did not answer but returned the pressure on my hand, and when she closed her eyes tears came from beneath the lids.

Every head turned as I entered the church. The service had begun and the door opened with a heavy clang, distracting the reverent from Burder's uncompelling delivery. I avoided all eyes, went straight to my pew and knelt. There have been times when my prayer had been for a better Vicar. Not better in the spiritual sense, poor Burder is laden with the inner qualities, but for a man who could lead me. He was holding forth on wickedness and the saving of the soul for the repentant and I, stricken with wrong-doing, ached for forgiveness. When I opened my eyes they were drawn to Madeleine's place. I would have given the remainder of my soul to have seen her bowed there, feasted my eyes upon her inch of bare neck bent in meditation. I saw one girl whispering to another, a cadet looking towards a pupil who seemed from a distance to be returning his attention. I saw Edwin Reed taking out his folded handkerchief and removing a piece of cake from it which he consumed with evident pleasure. In the pauses I heard his grunts. In my mind there was another picture. Of Madeleine. She rose from the bed and tried to dress, to leave my house before I returned to it. Blood coursed down her white legs and grew in a pool on the floor. So real was my vision that as Burder descended from the pulpit I leapt to my feet and fled the church, leaving them no doubt agog at my departure as they had been when I arrived. I am sure I left the door gaping wide.

She was on the floor. I have never believed in the supernatural but it seemed at that moment I had been given a power beyond my senses for she lay as I had imagined, the nightshirt I had lent her soaked with blood, her legs slippery with it. She was conscious and held out her arms to me. 'My poor girl,' I whispered. There was so little that could be done. I put her back onto the bed and raised her legs with books which I piled high. I staunched the blood with towels, and then sat beside her, holding her hand. Her mind was wandering. She motioned to me to bring my ear close, and said to me, 'I love him so much.' Then she attempted to raise herself, saying frantically that she must go to the cave where he was waiting for her. I told her she could not go now and she said that I must go for her. She drifted in and out of consciousness, each time she awoke she begged me to hurry, making me assure her that I knew where to go. She reverted to French. 'Down the slope, by the lake edge. Do you understand? Do you know the place?' I answered her in her own tongue. 'I know where it is.' Then she said, and the words ring in my mind so clearly I am deluded that it is her voice I hear. 'I would not have done this if he had not taken Dolly out to tea. I'm sorry now. Tell him to wait.' Her hand was cold in mine and I said aloud, 'I will tell him to wait.' I sat there by her for God knows how long, my eyes on her face.

8.39 p.m. She has been seven hours in Eternity. I performed those necessary functions to the body and, like the murderer I am, was disposing of the bloody evidence when there was a hearty knocking at the door. Mrs Burder stood smiling on the threshold, offering me a ride to the school in the pony trap. It was indeed parked just beyond my gate, with her children hanging over the side to look and the Vicar holding the reins and the whip. He raised the latter in greeting to me calling out that he hoped I was ready for the Hunt. I must have stared blankly at her for she reproved me for having forgotten and not for not listening to her husband when he gave out the time in church that morning.

I declined her offer. She urged that I should support the girls in their good cause and seemed chastened when I thanked her again and informed her that I was unwell and could not come. I posted myself at the window and watched almost the entire population depart for the Easter Egg Hunt. Miss Vernon rattled off with an assortment of children in their Sunday best. Edwin Reed pedalled perversely across the roughest terrain. When the Green was deserted and my watch told three, I wrapped Madeleine in her cloak and with my dawn ride a grim rehearsal for the present act, I rode her out of the village with a daring I did not know I possessed, short of war. I could not be certain that prying eyes were either closed in post prandial sleep or seeking out painted eggs a mile away, but I told myself that if I were seen, then God willed it and it was my just dessert. I would confess my sin. Further, I would compound it, to spare *her*. I would swear that I had forced her to submit to my carnal desires, that I was responsible not only for her death but for the beginning of that life which I had terminated. However, God was my only witness as I crossed the Green, and from then on I bore my sad burden over ditches and through thicket until I reached the gate that opened onto the lake path. I tied up my trusty mount, and with some difficulty heaved down the corpse and in my arms transported it to the cave to which in her last moments she had directed me.

But first I concealed her in the undergrowth and went in to investigate. That it had been a trysting place was evident, half candles on a low crevice, a blanket covering the floor. I thought of my mistress's comfortable flat in Maida Vale before the war and my heart ached for the lovers who had pledged themselves here. Both gone. Madeleine and Will. A spider ran across the wall and I recalled some country law that certain species have numerous pairs of eyes. Well, I thought, I don't know how long you've lived in this cave but you have seen a drama which will end here too. I went outside to bring her in and other eyes confronted me – those of Edwin Reed as he urinated against a tree, a basket of gaily coloured eggs on the ground at his side. What had he witnessed? It mattered not. He could betray me no more than the spider. I thanked God for giving him a cleft palate and a simple brain. I waited nevertheless until he set off in answer to a blast on a whistle, and then interred my only love in her tomb.

I stayed with her until dusk. The strength I had acquired (and I believe it to have been miraculous) ebbed from me, drained out of me like Madeleine's blood. I crouched on the damp floor close to the grave nature had provided. The cave might have been constructed to receive a slender corpse, for the roof sloped down at the back leaving a cubby hole just long enough to receive a tall girl (an estimated five feet eight inches) and low enough to leave no more than six inches between the body and the rock. I had protected her as best I could. I had no winding sheet but I had taken the blanket on which she must have groaned her pleasure and rolled her in it. It was an extra layer for the rats to bite through. I heard them leave, the Easter Egg Hunters. Throughout the late afternoon voices reached me, the shrill girls as they cleared away the entertainment, the rougher accents of the local men who (I now know) had been called in to search. I heard heavy boots approaching, the susurration of the long grasses as they were thrust aside. I thought, it is all up with me and like a hunted animal I froze in my bolt hole and watched as the yellow glow from a lantern cut across walls and missed me by a centimetre. Somnolent moths catapulted into action along the beam and thudded against the glass shield like exploding shells. Then the light withdrew and he who had withdrawn it continued his path with such a measured tread I named him as our stalwart guardian of the law, young William Best, who had been brought squealing into the world by my father after a long labour. I remember my father returning home saying 'A strapping fellow, but he was reluctant to face the harshness of this life.'

11.51 p.m. The day is almost out. I had been writing while still wearing my outdoor clothes although I had had the good sense to put a light to the fire. That I had not attended to the lamps is witnessed by the uneven hand. My pen drew me after it until the flames were too low to see and the moon had not yet reached my window. I think I should have spent the night in my chair had the telephone bell not summoned me from the recesses of the cave where Madeleine lay. It took me some moments to recover myself, remember my whereabouts. It was like waking in a strange room, unorientated. I went out into the hall and placed the trumpet to my ear. I think I said, 'Ford speaking.' It was Marie begging me to come at once to the school. I could not make head nor tail of her story, only that Madeleine had not been seen since morning and that one of her girls had been taken ill. At first I said I would not go. I could only think it was a trick to get me there, that they would confront me with the body, laid out by knowledgeable hands, no common murderer this, all evidence evincing my guilt. I saw myself strung up, neck snapping, feet pedalling the air. 'Please come,' wept the persistent Mrs Pennington, who will trap me one way or another, 'I have no other friend to turn to.' Doctor Chevington? He, as luck would have it, was already out on a case. Madeleine had trembled as she had climbed upon the table in her sheet. 'I am unnerved,' she said, and I clapped the ether pad over those white lips to still her fears. I was 'unnerved' too, and I trembled so as I shaved my beard I thought I might cut my throat. I put on a laundered shirt and my pressed breeches and I took my mare and rode up the drive of Fairwater House, expecting the ghost of Will Kent to bar my way and accuse me of slaughtering his mistress and his child.

It was not a phantom who waved me to a halt but a red-faced bombardier with a storm lantern held aloft. He shouted at me to pull aside and hold my horse, and I scarcely had time to obey him before a gun was dragged across my path by half a dozen soldiers and shoved and pulled towards the grassy slope that inclines down towards the lake. 'Bad business,' said the bombardier as I dismounted, and advised me to tether my mount in the stable yard. I did as he suggested, then, with sickening apprehension, I approached the house.

They had been summoning up her spirit, that group of hysterical maidens to whom I administered stern words and a bitter sedative. I, who discounted country tales of the occult, had become as credulous as a girl myself, half afraid that her voice might have reached them from the grave – or in this case *cave*. Had she made known to them that I had raped and robbed her with a curette? I left them to Matron who was shocked to her starched soul and closeted myself with Madame. Her anguish cut into me with the finality of the above mentioned instrument and scoured around

138

my battered heart. How I dissembled and lied! How I cheated and suffered for her grief and mine. I comforted her, chided her and prescribed warm milk to enable her to sleep. I forced my gaze to a sketch of Madeleine that had been disinterred to aid the police in what I prayed would be a thankless search. I had deprived my friend of her ward because blind love had overcome a lifetime's scruples, had overwhelmed my judgement and destroyed our lives, Madeleine's, her child's, Marie's and mine. I had sinned against nature and I concealed it with deceitful words that were lost in the roar of the cannon as it sent forth fire to raise the body that certainly was not lying in the lake.

I wished now that I had not found the answer which once I had so diligently sought. I had all but finished the dreadful testimony when Ida's voice brought me back to the present, calling out that the evacuees had arrived, where was I, I was needed downstairs.

Ida! Well, we were all in our way responsible, we had all played a part. I did not know what I should do with my knowledge, whether I should take the diary and destroy it or present it to the police. But who would care, with all our daily casualties, about a French girl who had been missing twenty-three years before? Doctor Ford had kept his secret – or had he? I thought of his widow, respectably retired in a hotel among the Bournemouth pines, the woman he said would trap him 'one way or another.' Why harm her now?

'Are you there, Miss Dolly?'

'One minute, Ida. I'm just coming down.'

I turned to the last page and a snapshot which had been adhering to the paper detached itself and fluttered to the floor. I bent to pick it up and for a few moments the fading image saddened me more than the story I had read. Florrie had never been a good photographer. Shadow made indistinct features I could not quite recall, but Madeleine's hair was lit like an aureole. She was leaning forward, painting an egg.

I placed it back carefully between the pages. Tears blurred my vision but the writer had little left to say.

An Easter Egg Hunt and much else is over. It is now two hours after midnight, the terrible day has gone. Monday the fifth of April is dawning. Christ is risen and Madeleine is irrevocably dead.

NOW READ ON . . .

The PAVANNE list exists to bring to the reader a paperback collection of acclaimed, entertaining and individual novels which might otherwise be left to languish in small expensive hardback editions. They are not the best-selling 'blockbusters' and formula romances usually found in women's paperback lists. They are true novels – absorbing, well written, by men and women, some established, some introducing new talents – poignant, witty, suspenseful, always appealing to the reader who considers herself to be a romantic in the true sense of the word. Each one is different to the last yet they all have one thing in common: quality fiction.

Pavanne's provocative list of writers for the future include:

Nora Ephron whose witty roman-a-clef *Heartburn* about the break-up of her marriage to Watergate journalist Carl Bernstein was a huge success in America.

Bel Mooney – Sunday Times columnist whose first novel is entitled *The Windsurf Boy*

Charlotte Bingham – whose new book *Belgravia* recaptures for the Eighties the style of her Sixties bestseller *Coronet Among the Weeds.*

Leslie Caron – actress and dancer, star of *Gigi, The L-Shaped Room* and *An American in Paris* has chosen to write her memoirs as fiction in her first book, *Vengeance.*

Marge Piercy – about whose new book *Fly Away Home* an early review states "she is one of those rare writers who can take such stock material as a woman's liberation and radicalization and move it out of ideology and into absorbing fiction"

Also available in Pavanne

K. M. Peyton
Dear Fred

A captivating novel from the creator of Yorkshire TV's long-running *Flambards* serial.

In Newmarket in the 1880s, young Laura cherishes (along with the rest of England's female population) an ardent attachment to Fred Archer (still the greatest jockey of all time, who tragically committed suicide aged twenty-nine), spending more time in her uncle's stables than in her own somewhat Bohemian home.

K. M. Peyton has taken the drama of Fred Archer's real-life achievements and mixed with it some beautifully interpreted fictitious characters to make a magnetic and finally heart-breaking story.

'Warm-hearted, richly-endowed with exciting scenes and with utterly believable characters' SUNDAY TIMES

Gail Godwin
Violet Clay

The author of *A Mother and Two Daughters* tells the story of Violet Clay, an artist who earns her living illustrating fleeing heroines on the covers of Gothic novels while still managing to persuade herself that one day she will become established as a serious painter.

Skilfully blending past and present, Gail Godwin unfolds the dilemma and resolutions of a woman's battles with her life and work. With elegance and sharp perception she captures the pain and frustration of a woman trying to come to terms with her past life, and, at the same time, seeking to construct a future.

'Gail Godwin has produced an honest and appealing tale. An excellent, sharp and invigorating book' *Spectator*

Jane Beeson
A Winter Harvest

Both Fay Weldon and Erin Pizzey have remarked upon the extraordinary power in Jane Beeson's writing. She lives on a remote farm on the Devon moors which forms the background for her first novel *Apple of an Eye* and the BBC television drama, *A Winter Harvest*, for which she has written both the scripts and the novel currently available in Pavanne.

A Winter Harvest tells the story of Caroline (played by Cheryl Campbell), a rather dreamy girl given to writing poetry, raised in a city, who marries Patrick, a farmer, and goes to live with him on his remote moorland farm.

When Patrick goes into hospital Caroline has to run the farm on her own through one of the bleakest winters ever, a role for which she is ill-equipped.

Caroline's attempts to come to terms with her feelings of isolation and inadequacy make *A Winter Harvest* a unique insight into the life of a woman in the countryside of the Eighties.

Pavanne

A complete list of titles in print

☐	Before She Met Me	Julian Barnes	£1.75
☐	Pas de Deux	Olivier Beer	£1.25
☐	Apple of an Eye	Jane Beeson	£1.75
☐	A Winter Harvest	Jane Beeson	£1.75
☐	Wish Her Safe at Home	Stephen Benatar	£1.75
☐	A Matter of Feeling	Janine Boissard	£1.75
☐	Forever Young	Ray Connolly	£1.75
☐	The Secret Keeper	Shirley Eskapa	£1.75
☐	An Easter Egg Hunt	Gillian Freeman	£1.75
☐	The Marriage Machine	Gillian Freeman	£1.75
☐	Violet Clay	Gail Godwin	£1.75
☐	Sweet Lies	Diana Hammond	£1.50
☐	Angel Landing	Alice Hoffman	£1.50
☐	Property Of	Alice Hoffman	£1.50
☐	White Horses	Alice Hoffman	£1.95
☐	John and Mary	Mervyn Jones	£1.50
☐	The Death of Ruth	Elizabeth Kata	£1.25
☐	Columbine	Raymond Kennedy	£1.75
☐	Going to California	David Littlejohn	£1.75
☐	My Old Sweetheart	Susanna Moore	£1.75
☐	Tim	Colleen McCullough	£1.75
☐	Dear Fred	K. M. Peyton	£1.50
☐	A Married Man	Piers Paul Read	£1.95
☐	Jules and Jim	Henri-Pierre Roche	£1.50
☐	The Intruder	Gillian Tindall	£1.95
☐	Peacefully in Berlin	Patricia Wendorf	£1.75

All these books are available at your local bookshop or newsagent, or can be ordered direct from the publisher. Indicate the number of copies required and fill in the form below.

Name _____
(Block letters please)
Address _____

_____

Please send to Pan Books (CS Department), P.O. Box 40, Basingstoke, Hants.

Please enclose remittance to the value of the cover price plus: 35p for the first book plus 15p per copy for each additional book ordered to a maximum charge of £1.25 to cover postage and packing. Applicable only in the UK

While every effort is made to keep prices low, it is sometimes necessary to increase prices at short notice. Pan Books reserve the right to show on covers and charge new retail prices which may differ from those advertised in the text or elsewhere